HARRY HARRIS

CUTS LOOSE

HARMONY HARRIS

CUTS LOOSE

JENNY OLDFIELD

Hodder
Children's
Books

a division of Hodder Headline Limited

A Catalogue record for this book is available
from the British Library

ISBN 0 340 87919 X

Typeset in Palatino by Avon DataSet Ltd,
Bidford-on-Avon, Warwickshire

Printed and bound in Great Britain by
Bookmarque Ltd, Croydon, Surrey

The paper and board used in this paperback by
Hodder Children's Books are natural recyclable products
made from wood grown in sustainable forests.
The manufacturing processes conform to the
environmental regulations of the country of origin.

Hodder Children's Books
a division of Hodder Headline Limited
338 Euston Road
London NW1 3BH

Her godmother touched her with her wand, and at the same instant her clothes were turned into cloth of gold and silver, all beset with jewels; after this she gave her a pair of *Glass Slippers*; the finest in the world.

Being thus dressed out she got into her coach; but her godmother above all things, commanded her not to stay beyond twelve a clock at night; telling her at the same time that if she stay'd at the ball one moment longer, her coach would be a pompion again, her horses mice, her footmen lizards, and her clothes resume their own form.

Cinderilla, or the Little Glass Slipper,
1697

One

It was a normal day. Wicked art lesson sticking bits of shiny green paper on to my 3-D lizard, boring science, a ruck with Tasha over bling.

Tasha (waving a picture of J-Lo under my nose): Guess what! Harmony Harris doesn't even know what bling means!

Me: Get lost, Tasha!

Tasha: Nah-nah!

Normal. Until I got home and they'd taken Mum to hospital.

Empty house. A note on the kitchen table – 'Come to number 72, love, Ruth.'

* * *

Empty house.

A cup of cold coffee beside the note, the door of the microwave standing open, Ophelia curled up on her usual cushion. I say 'empty', whereas I really mean 'no sign of Mum'. The cat was there, and the radio was still playing. But there was only the note. And I knew something was wrong.

I dumped my bag next to the mad cat and grabbed a packet of crisps. Eat when your world is about to turn on its head – that's my thing. Cope with a crisis on a full stomach. I read the note four times. Why did I have to go to number 72? Where was Mum? Why was there a cup of cold coffee on the kitchen table?

I munched prawn cocktail and stared at Ophelia. 'Did Mum have to go out for an audition?' I asked.

Cats don't answer even the most important questions. They only stare back through those weird black slits in the middle of their green eyes.

'I take that as a "no",' I said, scrunching the empty bag and tossing it at Ophelia. Cruelty to cats. Call the RSPCA.

Anyway, Ruth dashed down the street and found me.

'You're back!' she gasped.

I glanced down at myself – at my white school aertex and navy-blue skirt. 'Yeah,' I said.

'Your mum's in hospital,' Ruth told me. 'Kerry went with her. I said I'd stay until you got back.'

I frowned. 'What's wrong with her?' Mum was never ill. She doesn't believe in it. She sends me to school even when I'm dying.

Me: I've got a sore throat. It kills.

Mum: Open your mouth, say 'aah'. It looks fine to me. Off you go.

'Did she have an accident?' I asked Ruth.

She looked at her watch for an answer. 'No. She was being violently sick. She rang me and Kerry. We called the doc. He said to get her to hospital. Do you want to come in my car?'

So that's how I learned the bad news. There wasn't time to think or get scared. I was still in my school uniform, sitting in Ruth's rusty Corsa in a traffic jam on the Bristol Road, before it really hit me.

Ruth had told Ian next door to feed Ophelia, and where we were going and why. Ian has a grey ponytail and this habit of never looking at you when he speaks. Like he aims his eyes and misses. 'Okey-doke,' he'd said, taking in the cracked paving slabs on his front path, and the weeds growing in between. 'How is Jessica? Do they know what's wrong yet?'

'They're doing tests,' Ruth had said, giving Ian a look that said, *What kind of question is that when the kid can hear?* Everyone's eyes were sliding all over the place, I tell you.

By the way, you don't need to remember names like Tasha, Ian, Ruth and Kerry – they're just bit-part players. The main people come soon.

'Did you have a good day at school?' Ruth asked. We sat sandwiched between a

Sainsbury's lorry and a double-decker car transporter.

Mum was having hospital tests, and our neighbour could ask a dumb question like that.

An ambulance waah-waahed its way past, dodging from the bus lane to the outside filter, turning right past the uni towards the hospital.

We inched towards the junction and eventually followed the waah-waah siren.

Kerry met us in the hospital reception. 'Ward D,' she told us. We used the lift and went down long corridors.

'How is she?' Ruth asked.

People in white coats, green overalls, or blue uniforms criss-crossed the corridors. When I dared to look sideways into the wards I saw empty trolleys and wheelchairs, and plenty of full beds.

'They say she's comfortable,' Kerry replied. 'Whatever that means.'

Ruth gave her the look she'd given Ian. 'I'm sure she's gonna be fine,' she told me.

I should say right now that Mum's the only

person I've got in this world. No sisters and brothers. No dad.

We took a left, following an arrow that said Ward D. A woman wearing plenty of bling came out from visiting a friend or relative. A J-Lo lookalike. Just wait until I told Tasha-stupid-McClerran.

'She's in the far bed,' Kerry explained, whisking us past a place where the nurses sat, past patients sitting propped up on pillows, reading *Hello* and *OK*.

Mum had the pillows plumped up behind her. She wasn't reading. She was pale as anything. And she smiled at me like she was saying sorry.

'Did you feed the cat?' she asked.

That was Friday. I stayed over at Ruth and Kerry's, who we'd only known for a couple of months, but Mum liked them and she said anyway she planned to be checking out of that crummy place within twenty-four hours.

Some people think that Mum looks a bit of a wimp – she wears floaty skirts and burns scented candles, that kind of stuff. But I tell you, she's tough.

I'll pause here and give you a proper idea of her.

A quiet voice, I'd say. Slow and soft. Her voice is a really important part of her. She never shouts.

Big grey eyes, dark red hair, only she doesn't like you to call it red. Unlike mine, which you couldn't say was any other colour. Hers is long and straight. Mine's got a kink, which I hate. Mum's skin is smooth, she's got a small nose and a wide mouth. As you can tell, she's film-star good-looking, even though she's only played a couple of small parts in films. Mostly she works in the theatre or on telly. She's an actress. That's what she does.

You'd think she'd be vain, what with her hair and her face. And she wears size 10. But she's no way big-headed. When I was little she'd go out in the snow with me and build snowmen. She'd be wearing wellies and her hair would be stuffed up under her woolly hat. She'd always be laughing.

Or she'd be digging on her allotment, and me with my little trowel thingy. I'd always have my own patch for flowers and strawberries. I was OK so long as there weren't any worms.

Then she'd be off working for a few weeks in a theatre in York or somewhere, and I'd stay with Gran. Mum would write me a postcard every single day she was away. *'Dear Harmony, Did you water our lettuce? Don't let the slugs eat it all. Love, Mum.'*

That was before Gran died, when I was eight. Since then Mum's only taken work close to home, so she can be with me.

What else? Mum doesn't earn much money, so we don't have a car. She does office jobs sometimes, but it's acting she really likes. She called our cat Ophelia after a mad woman in a Shakespeare play. She talks to her in Shakespeare language – 'How dost thou, kitty? To be fed Whiskas or not to be fed; that is the question!'

Did I say she hugs me a lot, and calls me 'honey' in front of my mates?

End of pause.

* * *

So I stayed Friday night at number 72, then we visited Mum in hospital again next morning.

No way would she be checking herself out that day, a nurse told us.

Ruth had stopped at their station and asked how Mum was.

The ward sister (who was a man) used words like gallstones, drips, X-rays and scans. He smiled at me – the type of smile where your mouth just stretches but your eyes don't change. 'You look like your mum,' he told me.

Mum was sitting in exactly the same position as before. Only this time there seemed to be even more metal stands with squishy bags of fluid, and more tubes. She had dark circles under her eyes. 'I didn't sleep,' she told us. 'And they wake you up at six-thirty!'

'Are you still being sick?' Kerry asked.

Mum sighed and shook her head. 'Nothing left to be sick with.'

Yuck.

'Did you have a proper breakfast?' she asked me in her usual way.

I stayed most of the morning while Ruth and Kerry went off to the supermarket. Mum was tired and managed to sleep part of the time. I read a few mags and stared out of the window at hundreds of other windows.

'I could be in here for longer than I thought,' Mum made me jump by waking up and speaking while I was daydreaming.

I turned and I guess I looked miserable.

'Don't worry, it's nothing serious,' Mum said, trying to smile.

That's what they'd said about Gran at first. *Don't think about that!*

'It's just a nuisance,' she told me. 'Me lying here twiddling my thumbs, being poked and prodded.'

She was wearing a plastic bracelet with her name and number printed on. I'd brought in her one and only nightie – white satin with embroidery and bootlace straps.

She sighed again and held my hand. 'I think I might have to ring Uncle Marcus,' she said.

Two

Uncle Marcus is a name you'll have to remember.

He's Mum's brother, though you'd never guess it.

And before Saturday was over I was bombing down the M1 with him.

'I want to stay here with Mum,' I told them. I didn't mind sitting by her bed bored out of my mind. I wanted a relatives' room in the hospital, where I could stay and be near her while they finished the tests. Then we could go home to Ophelia and number 64 Norma Street.

'That isn't practical.' Uncle Marcus had

come on really heavy. 'It's much better if you stay with us.'

Mum had seemed so tired she didn't have the strength to argue. 'It's OK, Harmony, it'll only be for a few days.'

'What about school?' This question of mine shows you how desperate I was to stay. 'We start exams on Monday.'

'I'll be out before then,' Mum had promised.

'What about Ophelia?'

'Ian will carry on feeding her.'

'She'll be lonely in the house by herself.'

'Go home with Marcus and pack your bag,' Mum had insisted.

'But what about you?' I'd grabbed for her hand and nearly pulled out a needle by mistake.

She'd smiled in a tired way. 'You know me – I'm a tough cookie,' she'd said.

When I say you'd never guess that Uncle Marcus was Mum's brother, that's mainly because he has pots of money.

Well, not mainly, but it's the reason that hits you smack in the face.

Money. Probably millions, for all I know. Cars, a massive house. And you never see him out of a suit.

He came home with me to pack my bag.

'You won't need that,' he told me, taking my hair-dryer out. 'All our guest bedrooms are en suite, and they're fitted with these things as standard.' He looked down his nose at my battered trainers and combats, my manky T-shirts. 'Only bring what's absolutely necessary,' he ordered.

I insisted on taking six pairs of multi-coloured socks, including my Bart Simpsons, the ones where he's pulling down his trousers and mooning. I never wear a matching pair – always odd. I'm weird about socks. Oh, and I packed my too-small swimmie from when we last went on holiday. I stuffed them all in and flung them in the boot of his sports car. Think of the most expensive, six-cylinder, turbo-charged blah-blah, and it's that, with knobs on.

Uncle Marcus owns a factory that make important parts for central heating systems. He travels round a lot, like to America and

Japan. I think the factory's in India, but what do I know?

So there's the money and the job. Plus, he doesn't look anything like Mum. For a start, his hair's grey to match the suits. And he's fatter, and he shouts at his kids. I know this because I've heard him.

Uncle Marcus is married to Aunt Lucy – much more about her later, worse luck. They have four kids. They live at 12 Windsor Square.

This is who I'm going to stay with while Mum's hooked up to tubes and squishy bags, having her stomach and everything flushed out, and I'm in my uncle's Porsche (say Paw-sher), doing a hundred down the motorway.

'Hi, darling.' This is Uncle Marcus on the hands-free phone to Aunt Lucy. 'I'm north of Watford.'

'You're late,' Aunt Lucy says back. I can hear every word.

'Yes, well, something came up. Jessica's sick. I had to stop by in Birmingham at the Queen Elizabeth to see her.'

'What's wrong with her?'

'They don't know yet. It might be gallstones.'

'Isn't that what old people get when they drink too much?'

'That's gout. Anyway, they're doing tests. I'm bringing Harmony down with me.'

Long pause. 'How come?'

(Not, 'Oh great, that's fine by me. I'll get a bed ready for her. It'll be nice for the kids to have her around' et cetera.)

No, with Aunt Lucy it was just a long pause and 'How come?'

'Where else would she go?' my uncle pointed out.

Pause number two. 'For how long? You know we fly out to Florida next weekend.'

Uncle Marcus changed lanes like he was Michael Schumacher – vroom! 'Don't remind me. I've got a million things to do before then. Anyhow, I'm sure Harmony won't be a problem. Jessica will be out of hospital in a couple of days. It's probably just a bad case of food poisoning. Listen, darling, I have to make more calls. I'll see you soon. Bye.'

* * *

It was getting dark as we came off the M1 into London. You know the summer kind of dark, when the sky stays a bit light and people sit outside pubs. Uncle Marcus pressed a button and the hood of his Porsche came down, which meant we got all the petrol fumes and noise of the traffic. By this time he wasn't overtaking anyone or going anywhere above five miles per hour. Chug-chug. Cough-choke.

'Hi, Tom. Marcus. Did you get hold of that spread-sheet I asked you about? E-mail it to me straight away, will you?'

'Hello, I want to speak to Susan Mercer of Whitman and Parkes. Yes, I'm well aware that it's Saturday. This is Marcus Harris. Would you get her to come to the phone, please?'

'Tom. Marcus again. About the Kyoto deal. Get me the latest Dow Jones figures up on screen by tomorrow morning, OK?'

If this doesn't make any sense to you, don't worry. It didn't to me either. Uncle Marcus called twenty people while I read the neon hotel signs and breathed in car exhausts. I thought about how pale Mum had looked, whether Ophelia would miss us or not, the way the ward sister/brother (what do you call a sister who's a man?) had smiled without meaning it. Mum! I thought, with a fluttery feeling in the pit of my stomach.

We came through Swiss Cottage at a crawl. Then I think we passed a famous cricket ground, following signs to the West End. Around roundabouts with statues, past Hyde Park.

'Where are you?' Aunt Lucy came on the phone.

'About ten minutes away.'

Click. End of call.

I sat in the red leather seat wishing we could turn around and drive back to Norma Street.

12 Windsor Square isn't a house, it's a floodlit mansion.

Think big and white, with pillars and fancy carving, like a giant wedding cake. The iron gates swing open without you having to get out of the car, the tyres go crunch down a gravel drive.

Uncle Marcus parked the Porsche in the garage and went in by the side door. I followed.

'Finally!' Aunt Lucy greeted us. She looked at me and my bulging bag. 'Dinner's ready. Put that in the cloakroom, wash your hands and come into the dining room.'

(Not, 'Oh you poor thing, you look worn out. How's your mum? Let's show you where you'll be sleeping.' Anyway, you get the idea now without me having to keep on about it.)

Aunt Lucy didn't smile. She looked cross as she and Uncle Marcus disappeared out of the hall.

I'd only been here once before, when I was five. How was I meant to remember where the cloakroom was? I mean, there were about ten doors to choose from.

'In there!' a voice said from halfway up the stairs. It was my cousin Bryony, looking at me as if I was a monkey at the zoo, with a faint smile that says, *Look, she can stand on two feet and carry a bag at the same time. How clever is that!*

'Where?' I tried one door, but it was locked. I tried a second, into a room with a toilet and a wash basin. I closed the door, had a pee, still wished I was back at Norma Street. Washed hands, looked at myself in the mirror above the basin.

Hi, Harmony. How are you doing?

Rotten.

Why, what's up? You're staying in a mansion. You should be made up. I bet there's even a jacuzzi.

I don't wanna be here. I want to be with my mum.

Grow up, why don't you. Look, this gold mirror is worth more than your whole bathroom back in Norma Street. This is class, this is.

I want to go home.

Slumping my shoulders and letting my hands drip dry, I walked out into the hallway.

My four weird cousins were lined up on the stairs. I did mention them earlier, remember. They're called Luke, Bryony, Izzie and Jude. The Brain, the Brat, the Blub and the Blob.

'Be polite,' Mum had reminded me from her hospital bed. 'And try not to argue with your cousins.' She knows me and my big mouth.

The last time I saw Luke (the Brain), Bryony (the Brat) and Izzie (the Blub) was at Jude's (the Blob's) christening last November. Aunt Lucy and Uncle Marcus had a big party at some country house and they couldn't *not* invite us. Mum wore a way-out hat with feathers that a friend in the wardrobe department of the local rep had made specially. Bryony had told her she looked stupid in a loud voice.

'You're dripping on the floor,' the Brat told me now.

I wiped my hands on my combats.

The Brat smirked. She's only eight, but she's got this mega smirk.

Bryony Harris, eight years old, a junior version of Aunt Lucy. Enough said.

Luke Harris, twelve going on thirty. The Brain. He's away at school mostly, so I was *un*lucky to see him standing up there on the landing. If I say he's a geeky computer nerd who hates girls, you get the picture. Oh, and talk to him about fuel injection systems, low-profile tyres and real leather trims and he'll be happy, like his dad. Well, not happy. Luke never cracks a smile, the misery guts.

Which brings us to Izzie, the Blub. She sat on the stairs in front of Bryony, sucking her thumb and staring at me. Ellis-puff, Lizzie, Izzie. Real name, Elizabeth. She's three. Roly-poly legs and soft fair curls. She falls over a lot and cries.

Then there's Jude. This is a whole heap of new people to take in, but don't worry, there's not a lot to say about an eleven-month-old. He's the Blob – a big Buddha baby with rolls of fat and not much hair. He reminds me of the giant, man-eating plant in the 'Little Shop of Horrors' show that Mum was once in. *Feed me! Feed me!* A girl called Gabi looks after him, and she was standing on the landing next to the Brain, holding the Blob and smiling.

Yeah, smiling, like she was the only one who was glad to see me, and I'd never even met her before.

So that's hello to the rellys, with me as poor little Cinderella and no shortage of candidates for Ugly Sisters around the place. And I'll give you one guess for wicked stepmother. You won't see it yet, but Aunt Lucy gets that part, believe me. Clean that hearth, polish that grate, and no, you shan't go to the ball!

Three

Not that I was sitting in rags by the burnt-out cinders exactly.

My room was on the second floor. It had designer everything. There was a separate power shower, a whole wall with sliding doors that opened up into a wardrobe, a flat screen TV, cream carpet and white curtains. A tiny red security alarm winked in one corner of the ceiling, like an eye keeping watch.

'What are these?' Bryony demanded, unpacking my bag and pulling out Bart Simpson.

She ran off with my favourite socks, saying they were rude and she was going to tell her mum. I shoved my T-shirts on to a shelf and tipped my trainers into the bottom of the wardrobe. Then I went and pressed a few buttons in the shower room. A fan came on, lights went on and off, something blew hot air out of a vent in the wall.

Bryony came back minus Bart. 'Mummy threw them in the bin,' she said snidely.

'She can't do that!' I mean, they were *my* socks!

'She just did,' the Brat grinned. She took out my mini swimmie. 'What's this?'

I grabbed it fast. 'Nothing. Stop poking around in my stuff.'

'Hah!' Back came the smirk, which is where you curl your top lip and smile at the same time. It also involves your eyebrows – one goes up and the other cocks down. 'It's got frogs on!' Like this was the most disgusting idea in the universe – to have a swimming costume with a frog design.

I ignored her and turned my back, showing that I was above getting involved in a row with an eight-year-old.

While my back was turned, Bryony emptied out my hairbrush, gold scrunchy and copy of *Sugar* on to the king-size bed. 'Who's this?' she pestered, opening up the mag at a centrefold of Justin Timberlake.

Get this. The Brat doesn't know who Justin Timberlake is. My turn to smirk.

And another weird thing – Ellis-puff (the Blub) says all her words wrong and nobody bothers to put her right.

She says 'Har-mody' and 'Mwummy' and 'Uke'. Aunt Lucy ignores her and concentrates on Bryony. Uncle Marcus ignores everyone. I heard Gabi try to teach the Blub to say 'Harmony', but Gabi's a Romanian au pair, so her English isn't exactly perfect.

And *another* strange bit at the dinner table – Uncle Marcus's mobile went off and he answered it in the middle of his caesar salad. Aunt Lucy reacted like she'd been poisoned. She slammed down her knife and fork and glared at him. She didn't eat another bite.

Mind you, she's thin as string and lives on lettuce, so I suppose she didn't mind not having any of the meat course.

Uncle Marcus made it worse by getting up

and leaving the room for his chat about the Kyoto deal.

'Mummy doesn't like it when Daddy answers the phone,' Bryony explained over crème caramel.

By now Aunt Lucy had left the table in a strop. 'One day of the week for us all to get around the table and have a meal together,' she'd sighed. 'It's not much to ask!'

Izzie began sniffling, Luke was drawing patterns on the table-cloth with the prongs of his fork. Gabi went on spooning pudding into Jude's mouth.

'Why are your fingernails all chewed?' Bryony asked me in a loud, clipped voice.

OK, so I have weird cousins. I'm normal, right, and they're W-E-I-R-D.

And I don't just mean a little bit. I mean majorly Michael Jacko-Wacko.

I know for a fact, for instance, that Luke collects corks that have been popped out of champagne bottles by racing drivers who have won a Grand Prix. Nobody except him would collect stuff like that. Michael Owen autographs – yeah. Used champagne corks – well, what can I say?

I was thinking about this after I'd unpacked (with the Brat's so-called help), when the Brain knocked on my door and told me Mum was on the phone.

I shot downstairs in a nano-second.

'So you got there safely?' were her first words to me.

'How are you?' I gabbled back.

'OK, now they've taken some of those tubes out.'

'That's great. Does that mean you're better?' (How wrong can you be?)

'No, it just means they've re-hydrated me – topped me up with the fluids I lost when I was being sick. Listen, honey, some of the test results have come back. I was speaking to the doctor about them.'

'And?' I didn't like the pause that was hanging around in the air.

'They don't think it's gallstones after all.'

'Great.' This time I didn't really mean what I'd said. My voice sounded flat. 'Is it better or worse than that?'

Mum paused some more. 'It depends. They're saying it could be something to do with my pancreas. Pancreatitis.'

I'd never even heard of it.

'Apparently it's inflamed and they have to find out why.' Mum could tell I wasn't up to speed over this pancreas stuff. I mean, what was it? Where was it? What did it do? 'Let's let the doctors worry about it, shall we? But it means I have to stay here while they do more tests.'

Up until yesterday, the only tests I'd ever had to worry about were my SATs. Now I couldn't take a breath without hearing about the lousy things.

'Are you still there?' Mum asked in a tired voice. 'Harmony, let me speak to Uncle Marcus, there's a good kid.'

I put the phone down and went to get him. He took over while I sat on the bottom stair. 'Pancreatitis?' he repeated when Mum told him the news. 'My God, Jessica – how much alcohol have you been drinking lately?'

Afterwards, he went and told Aunt Lucy,

who didn't say anything because she was still sulking with him.

'P-a-n-c-r-e-a-t-i-t-i-s.' Luke wrote it down and went to look it up on the Internet.

Four

I know what it must feel like to win the lottery. From Norma Street to Windsor Square. From watching 'EastEnders' on a black and white TV with a Tesco's ready-meal on your lap to sitting in a jacuzzi in a private gym. And this had happened overnight. You blink a lot and pinch yourself on the arm to make sure you're awake and it isn't all a dream.

Or a nightmare.

Now sit up and pay attention. This is a whole section about me in a hot tub in my green frog cossie.

Uncle Marcus and Aunt Lucy have a gym in their basement. It has a rowing machine, a treadmill, weights, a sun-bed and a section with a sauna. Sunday is the only day it gets used because Uncle Marcus is out at work during the week, and Aunt Lucy has appointments with her hairdresser, her style guru, her personal trainer, her physiotherapist . . .

'The pancreas is a small organ next to the liver,' Luke told me as I sat amongst the jets and bubbles. 'It produces enzymes to absorb vitamins and minerals.'

Yeah, thanks Luke.

Bryony turned up the power in the jacuzzi. A jet of water blasted me in the small of my back.

'Pancreatitis is a disease of the pancreas,' Luke went on from memory. He straddled an exercise bike but didn't turn the pedals.

'Huh-huh-huh.' Uncle Marcus grunted as he rowed.

'It can be caused by a virus, but that's rare in this country. Usually it's from drinking too much alcohol.'

I took a deep breath. *But Mum doesn't drink!* I wanted to say. I left out a swear word because Aunt Lucy was lying on the sun-bed in goggles. 'But Mum doesn't drink!!!' Three exclamations marks instead.

'Wine, beer, whisky,' Luke insisted. '*Alcoholics* get pancreatitis. *Alcohol* destroys the tissue of the pancreas and it starts to decay.'

'Yes, thank you, Luke!' Aunt Lucy cut in. Like, *spare us the details*.

'Mum doesn't drink,' I repeated weakly. 'Anyway, we don't know it is that yet.'

Luke told us that his Google search had brought up all sorts of interesting stuff. You can live without a pancreas, but you have to take drugs all your life. You can never take another drop of drink, or it will kill you. The problem with pancreatitis is that your whole body gets poisoned by the decaying gunk inside you. They have to drain it out of your cavities with tubes.

'Thank you, Luke!' Aunt Lucy said in a tense, end-of-tether voice.

I started to think that maybe Mum drank in secret. Perhaps she had bottles of wine and gin stashed away in the cupboard under the sink, which she glugged in secret after I'd gone to bed. Then I got another blast from a water jet up my leg, and my swimming cossie blew up like a balloon.

Bryony sniggered.

The Brain got off the exercise bike and wandered among the weights without picking any up, which he definitely couldn't have done anyway. 'In the worst cases, the body stops being able to absorb nutrition from the food the patient eats. The patient gets dead thin and wastes away to skin and bone, but this can take months.'

At this point I considered getting out of the tub and clocking him one. But I was too embarrassed about my mini cossie all blown up with air bubbles. Even without the bubbles, it showed half my bum and the straps cut into my shoulders. Bryony's costume, by the way, was a trendy, snug two-piece in cerise and lilac.

I stayed put amongst the froth and the foam. Having considered then dismissed the secret drinking possibility, I went back to refusing to believe that Mum had anything wrong with her at all, let alone pancrea-thingy. *You wait and see – they'll let her out tomorrow, and everything will be back to normal*, I told myself.

'Was your mum in an episode of "Emmerdale" last week?' Bryony changed the subject, but only so she could do some more sniggering.

I shook my head.

'I'm sure it was her – the woman selling sausages at the farmers' market. She wasn't on for more than about three seconds, but it definitely looked like Aunty Jessica, didn't it, Mummy?'

I scowled.

'I take it Jessica's not working at the moment?' Aunt Lucy asked me from her tanning bed.

'Huh-huh-huh,' Uncle Marcus went.

'If she'd been working, it could have been even more awkward than it already is,' my aunt went on. 'Especially if she was filming. They would have had to bring in an understudy, or whatever you call them. And it's very expensive to re-shoot scenes.' Like she knew what she was talking about! And like Mum had got sick on purpose! My scowl turned into a glower, which is more seriously bad-tempered. Everything Aunt Lucy, Luke and Bryony said seemed to be getting at Mum in some way. She was ill. Why couldn't they leave her alone?

The tests will all be negative, I thought. *She'll be back home tomorrow, and I'll be out of here, da-dah!*

'Huh-huh. Tom says the Kyoto deal is looking dodgy,' Uncle Marcus gasped.

Aunt Lucy turned her head sideways. 'Marcus, don't tell me things like that. You know Miranda, my therapist, says I mustn't be subjected to stress!'

Uncle Marcus stopped rowing. 'Oh, we don't want to cause Lucy any stress! But the fact remains, Kyoto might be off. We may have to cut back.'

'I thought Tom said it was going through!' Taking off her goggles and putting on a dressing-gown, Aunt Lucy emerged from the machine.

'It was. Now it might not.'

'Cut back how?'

'Cut out the slack, y'know.'

'At work or at home? Because I can't do without Gabi. And I would never get rid of Anna. She's been cleaning this house for years. Good housekeepers are worth their weight in gold!'

'Don't worry, the cut-backs would be at work mostly,' Uncle Marcus snarled, and Aunt Lucy breathed a sigh of relief. 'But it would mean fewer holidays for us – no ski trip this year, for instance.'

Aunt Lucy tensed up. 'But Florida is OK? Marcus, tell me that we're still going to Florida. It's next weekend. You can't possibly disappoint the children like that!'

Bryony and Luke tuned in. 'Yeah, Dad, you promised we could go to Disney again!' the Brat whinged.

'Don't worry, your precious Mickey Mouse trip is safe,' Uncle Marcus grunted, grabbing the towel and stomping off. 'Anyway, we've paid up front, and it's non-refundable,' he added as he slammed the door of the gym.

Which left me fizzing away inside my

swimming costume, Bryony saying 'phew!', Luke lounging by the weights and Aunt Lucy deciding to blame me for something that hadn't even happened yet.

'It's so difficult!' she kicked off. 'This week of all weeks, when I have to plan for Florida – the very time when I could have done without a boring complication like having to take care of someone else's child.'

'Don't then.' This comment slipped out without me planning it. Me and my big mouth.

Aunt Lucy laid into me big time. 'Do you think I would if I had the choice? Marcus knows that I'm not keen on Bryony having to associate with you, even though you *are* her cousin. She could pick up bad habits, coarse language – anything.'

I let my mouth hang open – obviously one of my bad habits, but I tell you, I was gobsmacked. I didn't think even Aunt Lucy could come out with something as nasty as this.

'Close your mouth!' she snapped. 'And stop staring. Didn't your mother teach you anything?'

'Yeah!' Bryony agreed, suddenly turning off the jets and stepping out of the tub. She splashed me as she got out, which I should say was on purpose. 'Mummy says you talk like they do on "Crossroads"!'

I'm gawping up at them and they're dissing me. Luke is getting dangerously close to a smirk.

'I told Marcus last night that I didn't think your coming to stay was a good idea,' Aunt Lucy went on, jamming her black velvet Alice band more firmly behind her ears. 'From the second you arrived, I could tell you wouldn't fit in.'

What did I do? What major crime did I commit?

Aunt L was on a roll. 'I said to him, people can choose their friends, but they can't choose their families, more's the pity. Of course, it falls on deaf ears. He's so busy obsessing about doing deals and making money that he can't even spare five minutes for his family.'

I thought this was tough on Uncle M, since all the money he earned went on

39

paying for this luxury pad where they all lived it up.

Aunt Lucy would have been frowning, except that recent Botox injections must have paralysed those muscles in her forehead. 'I'm sorry to say this, Harmony,' (she wasn't) 'but Marcus knows full well that I don't approve of Jessica and the way she lives. All very fine to be Bohemian and chanting mantras when you're twenty, but it's quite another matter to bring up a child in that kind of weird atmosphere.'

Weird? Us? I breathed out hard through my nose. This meant I had to close my mouth, so that was one improvement as far as Aunt Lucy was concerned.

'And what do I get when you walk through the door? An unkempt, badly dressed urchin, a refugee from a car boot sale, a ... well, anyway, my first thought was, I can't possibly let you out looking like that. What would Bryony's friends think?'

I could go on with the insults that came my way, because Aunt Lucy must have spent about fifteen minutes on them. But you can see what had happened – she was in a bad mood with my uncle, so she took it out on me. Bryony and Luke listened in and practically clapped and cheered at the worst bits. If you think I'm exaggerating, you should've been there.

Mum says Aunt Lucy can't help being the way she is. She was brought up spoilt and she spoils her kids the same way.

She was a model when Uncle Marcus met her, and a pretty famous one. *Look at me – I'm tall, thin and incredibly beautiful!* That kind of thing. She still spends a lot of time in front of the mirror and hardly any on her kids. She's always asking herself, *Am I the richest, most beautiful woman on the block? Is that a wrinkle, a millimetre of fat?*

'She can't help it, she's trapped,' Mum says.

Mum's nicer about people than me. I think of Aunt Lucy as a kind of alien, or maybe the result of an experiment that's gone horribly wrong. Whoever made my aunt in the spooky Laboratory of Glamour forgot to give her a heart!

Here's a quick sketch of the Beanpole look – five foot nine, eight and a half stone, glossy dark hair, bambi eyes, make-up and a tan.

Bryony's a mini version, whereas Luke and Izzie look more like Uncle Marcus, minus the grey hair. It's too early to tell who the Blob takes after.

'Don't you have anything to say for yourself?' Aunt Lucy asked me after she'd run out of insults.

I was still submerged in the dead jacuzzi, trying to keep my cossie pulled down over my bum cheeks. 'I never asked to come here,' I told her.

She looked at me like I was something the cat dragged in. 'It's no good – you'll have to stay inside the house,' she decided. 'And if we have visitors you must go to your room.'

Fine by me.

'Let's hope your mother is better by the middle of the week at the latest,' was my darling aunt's parting shot as she flounced out of the gym with Bryony trotting after.

By this time Luke had achieved his smirk. 'How's it feel to be a charity case?' he asked me before he made his exit.

I wouldn't know. Charity is the last thing you find at Windsor Square.

Get better, Mum! I prayed in the dead silence. My fingertips were wrinkled as prunes when I finally staggered out of the tub. I pictured Ophelia asleep on her cushion, our pots of geraniums on the kitchen window sill. Who would water them while the house was empty?

Suddenly I was blubbing big style at the idea that the stupid flowers might die.

Five

You'd think it was a dream come true. It was Monday morning and I should've been getting up to do my maths exam, not lounging in my king-size bed listening to the Blob kick up a fuss. Let's be absolutely clear – I was missing an exam!!!

Luke had already left Harris Palace with Uncle Marcus, zooming up to the wilds of Northamptonshire, where he goes to school. My uncle was planning to drop him off then take the plane to Toronto.

Squawk-squawk. Jude wailed and bashed his spoon on his tray. I crept down in my South Park jamas to find Izzie snivelling into her empty cereal bowl and Gabi dashing around like a demented squirrel. The au pair brought cornflakes and milk for the Blub, then mashed some bananas into a mushy baby-slush for the Blob. She loaded Jude's spoon and guided it towards his mouth. Splat! Jude overturned the spoon and a gobful of his breakfast landed on the limestone flagged floor.

I slid into an empty chair at the table.

Good morning, Harmony. How are you? Did you sleep well?

No one said anything. Suddenly I'd become the Invisible Girl. So I helped myself to cornflakes.

There was more squawking and blubbing, then Bryony showed up.

'Is *she* still here?' she asked nobody in particular – 'she' meaning me. Bryony was dressed in a pink checked dress with a collar and a belt, her dark hair tied back in a glossy ponytail.

Gabi gave her a strawberry yogurt from the fridge.

'I want raspberry,' she said, *after* she'd torn the lid off.

Gabi went and got it for her.

Bryony ate two spoonfuls then chucked the pot into the sink. 'I want to leave now,' she announced.

Gabi wiped Jude down and picked him up out of his high chair. The Blob bawled some more. Izzie refused to move from her chair.

'*Now!*' the Brat insisted, secretly grabbing Gabi's car keys and stomping off.

No sign of Aunt Lucy, you notice. No, 'Bye, darling. Have a nice day!'

I chomped my cereal and kept my head down while Gabi scooted around with the Blob squatting on her hip. She took off his bib, found his mini trainers (aah!), brushed his head-fluff, then panicked. 'Come now,' she told Izzie. 'You must go to nursery school. But where is my keys?'

'The Bra— erm – Bryony's got 'em,' I muttered.

'Thanks.' With one quick check of her own reflection in the mirror in the downstairs cloakroom, grabbing Izzie by the chubby hand, she was gone and I was alone.

No phone call from Mum so far. But it was still only eight o'clock. Mind you, on Ward D they woke them up at six-thirty, so she'd had plenty of time to get in touch. Maybe all the gunk from her decaying pancreas had poisoned her like Luke said. Maybe she was in a coma, on a life-support system. My stomach clenched into a knot as my cornflakes turned soggy in the bowl. This was weird – I can never not eat, like I said earlier.

You get thirty per cent of your daily intake of iron from a bowl of cornflakes – not many people know that.

A key turned in the lock and a stranger came in through the side door.

This, it turns out, was Anna. Anna the Demon Duster, the Holy Housekeeper. Thou Shalt Not Make a Speck of Dirt!

Anna is ancient. She's been cleaning houses all her life. What Anna doesn't know about polishing, vacuuming, stacking dishwashers and ironing isn't worth knowing. She's small and thin, clean and pressed, with neat grey hair and lower legs encased in thick tan tights. Her legs don't quite fit the rest of her body, in that they're sturdy and look like they belong to someone bigger, like a rugby scrum-half for instance. Phew! I'm spending time on how she looks because the way she glared at me in that first moment wasn't nice – like I was something Ophelia had dragged in. Anna made a bad impression on me, right from the start.

She moved like a tornado, whisking bowls and plates from the table, whirling the dishes into the dishwasher, deliberately ignoring me.

Yep, I was definitely the Invisible Girl.

The housekeeper pressed buttons then listened to the swish of water jets inside the dishwasher – obviously music to her ears. After that she filled a yellow bucket and mopped the floor, bit by bit, without missing a square centimetre, concentrating on the sticky spot where the Blob had ditched his breakfast. I sighed and backed out into the hall.

Then it was out with the Dyson for Anna, sucking up dust that wasn't there on the stair carpet, driving me upstairs to my room, where I scrabbled in the wardrobe for jeans and a T-shirt. I'd only just got dressed when Captain Kleen marched in.

'Knickers!'

This was the first word she ever said to me, pointing to a laundry bin inside the en suite bit of my bedroom.

I grimaced – eyebrows puckered, mouth screwed tight – and shrugged.

'Dirty knickers, in there, not on the floor!'

'Yeah, got that.'

I received that look again, like I was road-kill.

'And anything else you need to wash,' Anna ordered. 'Don't try using the washing-machine yourself – you'll only break it.'

Listen, this woman didn't even know who I was, and she was treating me like dirt. Ha! Like dirt! Swish-mop-rub-scrub until you got rid of it.

I'm only a kid, but this was not a cool way to act, I knew that much. 'I'm Harmony

Harris,' I told Anna, looking her straight in the eye. 'My mum is Marcus Harris's sister.'

Well, this made things worse. Much worse.

'Ah!' she said, as if this explained how come this piece of low-life was here, and why I was cluttering up the place, dressed like a rag-bag, with wild hair and a common accent. 'You'd better stay in here and watch TV while I clean. I have my Monday routine and I don't want you getting in the way. And neither does Mrs Harris, I'm sure.'

'That's fine by me,' I said. I'd have done anything to keep out of my aunt's sight, short of an extreme sport like sky-diving (I don't like heights) or worm-digging (worm phobia). In fact, right that moment I was thinking of legging it back to Brum. Then I wouldn't be in anyone's way. Aunt Lucy would have a clear run to Friday and Florida.

I'd be at home with Ophelia, watering the geraniums, visiting Mum.

Ophelia's smooth and grey all over, with a long, thin tail and pale green eyes. One of the mad things she does it turn around in tight circles chasing her own tail.

Anna picked up the TV remote and handed it to me. 'Don't break it!' she warned, closing the door behind her.

Breakfast TV was still on. Someone was talking about kids' books being too scary and how you shouldn't include death. Kids were saying they didn't mind when things got squished in books. 'It was funny when the bird ate the worm. I liked it!' Me too. Worms are slimy and pink. They wriggle. Death to all worms!

Then they had people in a studio confessing that they ate chocolate in secret. They couldn't help it, they were addicted to Cadbury's creme eggs. Major tragedy.

What was the problem? I didn't get it.

But by now I should've been sweating over how many litres of water it takes to fill a swimming-pool measuring 10 metres by 20 metres, which starts at 80 centimetres at the shallow end and goes down to 2.5 metres at the deep end. I heard a car leave the garage and crunch up the drive. Gates opened and a silver four-wheel-drive BMW swished out.

A bit later, Gabi came back from the school run in a Fiat Punto with Jude, but minus Izzie and Bryony.

'You would like a drink?' Gabi knocked on the door of my room. Jude was still glued to her hip.

'Yeah, please.'

'What you like?'

'Orange juice.'

'Come down to kitchen. Is OK, Anna is cleaning Mar-coos's office.'

I grinned then she grinned back. I followed her downstairs.

A short pause for Gabi. Young, skinny and drop dead gorgeous. Long legs to die for, smooth skin, dark eyes.

So what's she doing here, skivvying for the Harrises?

She handed me my juice and I'd taken two gulps when Anna reappeared.

'How old are you?' she barked in my direction.

I looked round just to check. 'Me? I'm eleven.'

'Old enough to go to the shops by yourself, I would have thought!'

Anna has this knack of making comments out of nowhere. Like, 'Knickers!' And this one. Where did it come from?

I didn't know what to say, so I kept quiet.

'You'd think her mother could send her here with a set of decent clothes,' Anna fumed. You could practically see the steam hissing out of her ears.

'As it is, I have to break my routine and take her into town,' she huffed, talking at the microwave. 'Orders are orders, I suppose. And he who pays the piper calls the tune.'

Slowly I began to piece this together. It was nothing to do with actual pipers and everything to do with Aunt Lucy, who had driven off in her BMW. But before she'd gone she'd spoken to Anna and told her to make sure that I went clothes shopping. It turned out she was ashamed to have me in the house wearing what I'd packed in my bag, in case any of her friends spotted me. 'Buy her something halfway respectable,' she'd told Anna, who'd huffed and puffed about her dusting and polishing, but it had made no difference. Aunt Lucy was determined. 'And get her a haircut,' she'd added.

'I don't want new clothes,' I pointed out.

'And I don't want to take you,' Anna came back at me. I was road-kill, remember, and so not worth wasting money on.

Gabi sat nursing Jude. 'Go!' she told me. 'All girls love clothes. Have good time!'

Which is how I ended up on Oxford Street with the Dust Demon.

'Not those horrible combat trousers!' Anna told the assistant. 'She wants something smart and tailored, and not too grown-up.'

No, she doesn't! I pulled faces behind her back. *She wants slinky, strapless summer tops and baggy hipsters. She wants see-through vests and Diesel jeans!* And what I ended up with was a flowery thing from Liberty's, with a skirt, sleeves and a collar. Yes, you guessed it – a dress!! Aaagh!!!

'I'm not wearing that!' I yelped. I didn't know they still made them.

'You don't have any choice.' Anna took

me off to Clarks and stuffed my feet into white Jesus-sandals.

'Ouch!'

'They'll do!' she snorted.

Then it was Anna's time to finish work so we took the tube home. At least I escaped the haircut.

I went up to my room and blubbed. Honest.

When I came downstairs again, Aunt Lucy was back.

She'd been out to lunch for a lettuce leaf and half a tomato. 'There was a phone call from the hospital,' she told me, sourly taking in my still untamed kinks and curls.

My heart stammered and jolted to a stop. Then it juddered back into action. 'What did they say?'

'It's pancreatitis,' she confirmed in a flat, bored voice.

Everything went into slow motion. I saw Anna clutching a yellow duster, Gabi carrying Jude upstairs for his afternoon nap, a vase of white roses in the hall window.

'God knows!' Aunt Lucy sighed. She stared at me like it was my fault that Mum had a fatal disease.

'I want to see her,' I gasped.

'Well you can't. Marcus is away for the week, and I can't leave the children.'

'I need to see her.'

'It's not possible. Good God, we're going on holiday! And what am I supposed to do with you – pack you in my suitcase and smuggle you to Florida with us?'

I stared back. *Don't worry, I'm out of here!* Back up the M1 to Birmingham, with or without a lift from Uncle Marcus. I was mapping it out in my head – how I would catch the tube to the motorway then hitch a lift. That way I wouldn't need any money. *Mum's really ill! Ouch, ouch!*

'God knows what I did to deserve this,' Aunt Lucy ranted. 'Trust Marcus's blessed sister to come down with something like this at the most inconvenient time!'

I'd gone dead quiet, and probably pale.

My aunt shook her head at me. 'Don't look at me like that. Your mother's only got herself to blame. This illness happens when you drink too much – it's so shaming!' Slow motion. I saw Anna dust the banisters, Gabi come down and hover in the doorway.

Aunt Lucy was minus a heart, remember. 'Oh yes, Jessica's as poor as a church mouse and living in a place that's not much better than a squat, but she can still afford to buy alcohol and drink herself to death! I wonder how that happens!'

Gabi stepped forward. That's all I remember before I passed out.

Me fainting! I've never done it before, but suddenly Aunt Lucy's face went fuzzy and her voice faded. The whole room tilted. Click! My hard disk crashed and I was down.

Six

They put me to bed and called a doctor. The lady doc took my blood pressure and temperature, asked a few questions then went away.

I didn't see anyone else that evening except Gabi, after she'd put Jude and Izzie to bed.

'How you feel?' she asked.

'Rotten,' I croaked.

'It's gonna be OK.' Gabi smiled and patted my duvet.

No it isn't! I fought back the tears and made a clicking noise in my throat.

'Don't cry.'

Which made me blub again, of course. Gabi turned on the TV and stayed a while, until Bryony flounced in without knocking.

'What's the capital city of France?' she demanded.

'Paris,' Gabi told her.

I pulled the duvet up to hide my red, puffy eyes.

'Why is she crying?' the Brat asked.

'Because her mummy is sick.'

'You have to help me with my homework,' Bryony told Gabi. 'Now.'

Running away takes guts, no matter how much you hate a place.

And wow, did I hate Harris Palace.

I woke up on Tuesday to the same old thing – the Blob wrecking the place with his 'Feed me!' routine, Izzie crying for her 'Mwummy', Bryony dissing her because she couldn't say her words properly.

'You're not going to be sick, are you?' she asked me when she saw my pale face. 'Because if you are, Gabi will have to clean it up before Anna gets here!'

I'm trying to find something nice to tell you about the Brat, but I honestly can't. She's a spiteful, mean, cocky little so-and-so. I'm sorry, but she is.

I was glad when she went off on the school run with Gabi, because if she'd stuck around much longer I would've had a mega run-in with her.

But sitting alone in the empty kitchen made me start thinking of home. Timers clicked, machines whirred, lights winked. Uncle Marcus rang and left a message. 'Hi, it's me. I'm in Toronto. Lousy flight. Missed a connection. Tom says Kyoto's definitely off and profits are way down. Thought you should know. Speak to you later. Bye.'

I didn't want to be there when Aunt Lucy picked up the bad news, so I left the house and wandered across the road to a small park in the centre of Windsor Square. There were iron railings, trees, swings and roundabouts, benches to sit on. I chose a bench under a tree. *Concentrate. Make a plan. Get out of here!*

My mind wouldn't stick to the subject, which was Running Away. It slid off to watch a man and a boy playing footie on the grass. The boy was about three – Izzie's age. The dad was cool. What was it like to kick a ball in a park with your dad? Was it worse to have a dad like Uncle Marcus who never played with you, or not to have a dad at all, like me? Worse to have one who never played, I decided.

Then I watched the traffic. Black cabs, men on motorbikes, delivery vans, limos. It crawled non-stop down the street, around the square, down the next street, then the next and the next. That was a point – how was I going to find my way out of here? London was huge. Yeah, huge!

The tree dropped leaves on me. They floated down, light as feathers. I looked up and saw blue sky through silver-green leaves.

Last Friday I was a normal kid going home from school. That was years ago. Now I was sitting in a park all alone, feeling like everybody hated me.

'Say "Ta-rarr-a-bit!" ' the Brain had taunted before he went off to school. 'Go on, Harmony – everyone in Birmingham says "Ta-rarr-a-bit!" '

'Look at her tatty trainers!' The Brat had pointed at my shoes. 'I bet she got them from a car-boot sale!'

Actually, I didn't. But so what if I had?

The first thing they'd done after I arrived was hide my phone so I couldn't call Mum. That was their idea of funny. Ha ha – not!

'Here, take this,' Mum had said to me from her hospital bed. She'd handed over her mobile. 'I'm not allowed to use it in here. There isn't much credit on it, so don't go ringing all your mates!'

Then the Brat had laughed at my frog cossie, remember. And all this time Uncle Marcus and Aunt Lucy had let her. Not a peep out of them saying, 'Don't be mean to your cousin.'

I think they thought the Brat was wonderful and couldn't put a foot wrong. The same with the Brain. But I got the impression that Izzie was a bit of a disappointment – too roly-poly, too clumsy, always whingeing. And Jude – well, Jude had nappy-rash and sore gums. He was just one baby too many.

And me? Uncle Marcus didn't even register I was there. Aunt Lucy plain hated me. Hated me for nothing. Hated me for being me. For not being smart enough and posh enough. For being there.

Now why was that? I mean, why?

I was getting worked up into this mega strop when Gabi interrupted.

She came into the park with the Blub and the Blob. The Blob was in his pushchair and the Blub was hanging on to the handle and crying.

'Hi Gabi!' the cool dad called. He broke off from footie and came to meet her.

Gabi lifted Jude on to the grass and let him crawl around. Izzie hung back behind her as the footie kid ran across.

No one had seen me lurking under the horse chestnut.

The dad ran up to Gabi and kissed her.

OK, so that was why she skivvied for the Harrises and put up with all the hassle. He was smiley, with short, dark brown hair, wearing an O'Neill sweatshirt. It looked to me like they met up in the park pretty often.

'Wanna play?' the boy asked Izzie, holding up the football.

She shook her head.

'Yes, Izzie, play with Leo,' Gabi encouraged, as if she wanted alone time with her boyfriend. But instead of dumping her and leaving her to it, she bent down and took the ball herself. 'You kick, like this!'

The ball shot sideways and belted the boyfriend in the chest.

'Oof!' He staggered back like he'd been shot. 'Not like that, like this!' Carefully he placed the ball on the grass and showed Izzie how to kick.

'Kick!' Gabi said.

Izzie swung her roly-poly leg and missed. She sat down on her squidgy bum. Cool dad scooped her up and swung her round – wheee!

Izzie giggled.

I'll say that again. Izzie *giggled*!

Then she gurgled and laughed as her feet touched the ground. She ran after the ball and kicked again. Leo dived in a mega save.

'Go, Izzie, go!' Gabi and cool dad cried.

Jude crawled towards my tree. I shrank back, but Gabi turned and saw me. 'Hi, Harmony! Come play!' she called.

Well, I didn't fancy the idea, but what could I do? Before I knew it I was kicking the ball for Izzie – 'Fwetch da ball, 'Mody!' – and laying on passes for Leo.

'Good ball!' cool dad cried. He tackled his son and fell flat. 'Foul!' he claimed, jumping to his feet.

'Play on!' Gabi instructed. 'Shoot, Leo, shoot!'

This came as a complete surprise. There was I, one hundred per cent miserable, wondering if I was soon going to be an orphan and condemned to play Cinderella at the Harris Palace for ever, when the au pair shows up and does the Mary Poppins stuff.

Then I was smiling and laughing, down on my hands and knees crawling after Jude, giving Izzie piggy-backs. A spoonful of sugar, and all that.

I really liked Gabi. Think about it – she

took all that crud from Aunt Lucy, Luke and
Bryony – fetch this, carry that, do it now! –
and anyone else would've told them to stick
their job. But not Gabi. She didn't answer
back, she took good care of the baby, gave
Izzie lots of attention.

Oh, and it turns out that cool dad wasn't
cool dad – he was Leo's cool big brother. His
name was Joe, he lived in New Zealand and
was visiting his mum and her new family
over here in England. He was twenty – the
same as Gabi.

'When's your night off?' he asked her
when the little kids had run out of energy
and flopped on the grass.

She shrugged. 'Not this week.'

'How come?'

'Lucy and Marcus go on holiday Friday.
Everything very busy. Rush, rush, rush to
Disneyland.'

Joe faked a scowl. 'What about you? Is
Mickey the lucky guy?'

'Mickey?'

'Mickey Mouse. Does he get to date you
while you're at Disney?'

Gabi laughed. 'Oh no. I stay here. They borrow au pair from American friends in Orlando.'

Joe's face lit up as he spoke to Leo. 'You hear that, bruv? Next week we get Gabi all to ourselves!'

'Where's your new dress?' Aunt Lucy asked me after we went in from the park. 'Put it on, please, and don't give me any excuses.'

I put it on and looked at myself in the mirror. 1950s girl. Enid Blyton and the Famous Five. *Swallows and Amazons*. All I needed was a pet dog and a friend called Titty.

I was in full scowl when my aunt barged in.

'Don't think you can freeload off this family for ever,' she kicked off again. I guess she'd heard Uncle Marcus's message about Kyoto. 'Just because Jessica's ill doesn't entitle you to stay here *ad infinitum*, so don't think it does.'

I put on a dumb look.

'Don't be insolent,' Aunt Lucy snapped.

'There must be a dozen alternatives to you staying here – surely the State has some responsibilities in a situation like this. Don't you have a – a social worker – or somebody?'

I looked dumber.

'Don't worry, I'll look into it. Whatever Marcus says, I'm not putting up with this sort of behaviour from an eleven-year-old!'

Bang! The door slammed behind her.

I hope they have good, strong hinges on the doors at Harris Palace.

Tuesday wasn't Anna's day for cleaning.

At two o'clock Aunt Lucy went to watch Wimbledon with a friend. At three Gabi was due to take Izzie and Jude off to collect Bryony.

'Will you give me a lift into town?' I asked her.

'What for?' She took a pile of ironing off the laundry room table and carried it upstairs.

'I have to change these sandals,' I lied.

Listen, I didn't feel good about it, but I could hardly tell her I needed a lift to the tube station so I could get a ticket up to the M1, could I?

This is the way I'd figured it – car ride to tube station, study map of London Underground, buy a ticket, hitch a lift from the start of the motorway with a cardboard sign that read 'Birmingham'. I reckoned that by about eight o'clock I would be home. Mind you, I still knew that it took guts to get that far.

'What's wrong with the shoes?' Gabi asked.

'Too narrow. They pinch my feet.'

'Mrs Harris – she wants that you take them back?'

No eye contact, but I nodded.

'By yourself? Are you sure?'

Another nod. 'Can you drop me at Oxford Circus, please?'

I watched the Fiat Punto disappear up Oxford Street then ditched the naff sandals in the nearest bin, good riddance.

You could say I was travelling light, carrying only a tiny rucksack with my phone

(I'd sneaked it back from the Brat) and purse containing three pounds fifty exactly. Oh, and a rolled-up piece of card saying 'Birmingham'. I'd left my main bag in the wall-to-wall wardrobe at Windsor Square so as to avoid suspicion.

This is it – freedom!

But I was in a panic as I headed down the crowded steps to the tube. I was below shoulder height to most grown-ups, unable to see my way, so I just had to go with the flow. I was in a human river, swaying, jostling, bumping along. And this wasn't even rush hour.

Eventually the current dumped me by a ticket office where I found a map. Oxford Circus was marked with a million dirty thumb-prints. I knew the M1 was north, past a park. Would that be Hyde Park or Regents Park? I couldn't remember. And where was that cricket ground? Warren Street, Euston, Camden Town. The names might have been in a foreign language for all I knew.

Someone shoved me in the back with an

elbow, a giant suitcase crushed against my shins. This was scary.

Then I saw two school kids in green uniforms, laughing and joking as they slid their tickets into the machine at the barrier to the Central Line. No problem. If they could do it, so could I!

But which line? Central or Bakerloo? Then how far, and where would I change lines? What if I kept on going round in circles until they threw me off? And where did I actually want to get to? I still hadn't worked that one out. My mouth went dry, my hands grew sticky. The air down here was muggy and I felt I couldn't breathe.

'You OK?' a woman with a London Underground badge asked.

I nodded and dived for the stairs up to Oxford Circus, emerging into the air like a gasping fish. But then I didn't recognize any of these shops. Was this the place I'd gone down from? No, that was across the intersection. Now I was really confused. And the streets were getting more and more crowded and noisy. Horns hooted, exhaust fumes pumped out, a double-decker bus careered past me.

Help!

I sound like a wuss, I know.

But these were people with places to go, never looking at each other, pushing, shoving, shuffling. There was a beggar with a dog and a blanket sitting outside a Miss Selfridge and a man selling newspapers from a tiny booth. Maybe he would know the way to the M1. I went to ask him but he looked down at me like I'd totally lost it.

'Forget it, darlin',' he said.

Not yet. I might be clueless about tube stations, but I wasn't about to give in.

'Hi, it's me, Harmony,' I said above the roar of a passing lorry.

'Harmony, where are you?' Ruth's voice answered the phone. Ruth from 72 Norma Street, remember? She was top of Mum's Phone Book list.

'I'm at Oxford Circus,' I told her. 'Listen, I'm coming home.'

'Who's with you?'

'No one. I want to see Mum. I hate it here.'

I thought Ruth would understand, I honestly did.

'How are you getting back?'

'Hitching,' I said, like you might say 'taking the dog for a walk'. 'Only I can't find the motorway.'

'Right.' Ruth sounded dead efficient. 'Listen, Harmony, don't move. I'll sort it out and ring you back.'

'Will you look at a map for me? I need the nearest tube station to the motorway.'

'Yes, OK. But listen, which shop are you standing near?'

'Miss Selfridge.' Like a fool I told her.

'Give me half an hour. And stay exactly where you are.'

I suppose I was expecting Ruth herself to turn up in her clapped-out Corsa, or a special police escort up Oxford Street. Don't ask me, I didn't think it through.

In fact, if you gave marks out of ten for running away, I'd definitely have scored *nul points*!

Seven

Look, I'm only eleven, and I've never had to run away before!

OK, so my idea didn't have a snowball in hell's chance of succeeding, but at least I tried.

'Harmony, it's not clever and it's not funny!' Aunt Lucy said when she picked me up at Oxford Circus.

I didn't for a nano-second think that it was.

That Ruth was a real traitor! It turns out she called Mum in the Queen Elizabeth, who called Uncle Marcus, who called Aunt Lucy, who came to fetch me.

And wow, was my aunt in a bad mood!

'If it had been up to me, I'd have chosen to

leave you where you were and let you fend for yourself. But no – Marcus seems to think he has to show family solidarity, even though you turn out to be the most ungrateful little wretch on God's earth!' She stalled at the lights, fumed over the traffic jams, tapped her icing-sugar pink fingernails on the steering wheel. ' "Good riddance!" is what I said to Marcus. I told him it was obvious you didn't want to stay with us, and we certainly don't want you there, do we, Bryony?'

By this time the insults were running like water off a duck's back. I sat in the car, staring out at the big shops, feeling bad about what I'd done to my poor mum. I pictured her taking Ruth's phone call in hospital. Major panic – one daughter lost in the centre of London. Anything could happen – I could walk under a bus, get abducted by a stranger, anything. Mum calls her brother in Toronto, he goes mental, calls his wife. She has to cancel her Pilates class to come and fetch me.

'Can I call Mum?' I asked as we swept

through the automatic gates at Windsor Square.

Aunt Lucy got out of the big BMW and slammed the door. 'Don't you think you've done enough damage for one day?'

Which meant, 'No, you can't phone her.'

'Have you rung her to say I'm OK?'

Up went the eyebrows, the lip curled. 'A pity you didn't think of that sooner!'

The Brat launched herself out of the car. 'Yes!' she agreed. 'A pity you don't have a brain, Harmony Harris!'

Ha ha! I'd never felt so miserable as at that moment when I stepped back inside Harris Palace. The big door closed behind me, the scent of the white roses in the hall enveloped me – the smell of what for me seemed like prison.

There were real paintings on the walls, plasma TVs, surround-sound, French windows, carved cupids and antique vases, but so what, if it came along with my bitter and twisted aunt and my spoiled-rotten cousins?

* * *

'Don't let her out of your sight!' Aunt Lucy ordered Gabi. 'Take her with you to Bryony's tennis coaching session. Make her stay in the car and lock her in.'

Bryony was upstairs getting changed when the phone rang. Gabi answered it then handed it to my aunt.

'Yes, hello, Jessica,' Aunt Lucy said wearily. Tap-tap went the pink fingernails on the hall table. 'Yes, she's back. No, she didn't come to any harm.'

I held my breath and bit my bottom lip.

'Lucky for you that you have a halfway sensible neighbour,' Aunt Lucy went on. 'Jessica, have you any idea what a dangerous stunt your daughter just tried to pull? One eleven-year-old girl alone in the middle of Oxford Street! Imagine the headlines if anything had happened. And it would have been Marcus and me who would have taken the blame! . . . What? Yes, she is here . . .'

Let me talk to her! I prayed.

'Do you think you're up to it? Jessica, you're sounding quite tired and overwrought.

And I'm not sure if Harmony deserves to speak to you after what she's done. Of course, that's been the problem all along as far as I'm concerned – not enough discipline in her life since she was very small. I always said that you gave her too much freedom, and now you're suffering the consequences . . .'

Let me talk to my mum!

'Calm down, Jessica . . . it's against my better judgement, but here she is.' Aunt Lucy thrust the phone at me and flounced off.

'Harmony?' Mum sounded shaky, like she'd just been shouting.

'Yes. Mum, I'm really sorry!' My own hand was trembling as it held the phone to my ear.

'What got into you?'

'I don't know. I was worried about you. I want to come and see you.'

There was a long pause. 'I told you not to worry – I'm gonna be fine. Anyhow, Marcus will probably drive you up to the hospital this weekend.'

'He can't,' I told her. 'They're going to Disney.'

'Oh.' Another long pause. 'That's nice. Are they taking you too?'

'No way!' Bryony's voice butted in. She'd picked up an upstairs extension and been snooping in on our conversation. '*She's* not coming with us!'

'Sounds like that's a no,' I told Mum. Not that Aunt Lucy had actually bothered to tell me what was happening when they went away.

Mum sighed. 'Don't worry, I'll talk to Marcus.'

'I don't want to go,' I said quickly.

'You can't come anyway!' Bryony cut in.

'So how are you feeling?' I asked, to change the subject.

'Better,' Mum said, though she didn't sound it.

'Maybe they'll let you out by Friday.'

'Yes, maybe.'

'Mum, if they don't, why can't I stay with Ruth and Kerry?'

'Because they have work and lots of stuff

going on. And I don't know them that well, so it's not something I'd like to ask them to do.'

By this time she was sounding really tired. It didn't feel right to pester any more. 'OK, I'd better go. You talk to Uncle Marcus.'

'Tomorrow,' she promised. 'I'll call you soon.'

'Love you,' I told her.

'Love you too,' she told me back.

'That's my cousin from Birmingham,' the Brat told all her mates at tennis.

I was sitting on the sidelines watching them whack balls into the net. Gabi had refused to lock me in the car.

'Why is she staying with you?' one girl asked, giving me the monkey-in-the-zoo look. I'd been forced back into the flowery dress.

Bryony trotted to fetch a ball from the back of the court. She hit it at me, accidentally on purpose. 'Because she's poor. Her mother can't afford to pay someone to look after her.'

'Where is her mum?' Bryony's mate talked

about me as if I wasn't there. She had all the gear – the Venus Williams halter-neck dress, the flashy racquet.

'She's sick,' Bryony replied. 'I don't know. Don't ask me.'

Whack-whack! Six more balls hit the net.

'Backhand drive!' the female coach announced. 'Get your feet in position, ready to receive.'

A dozen mini tennis players crouched low. Whack-miss-whack-plop. Their parents were paying a fortune for this.

'Move your feet, Bryony!' the coach yelled.

The Brat scowled. 'Tell her to move back!' she muttered, pointing in my direction. 'She's putting me off!'

That was Tuesday – the day I ran away. Wednesday was back to normal – Anna cleaning and polishing like a maniac, looking as if she still wanted to suck me up into the Dyson, Aunt Lucy going for a foot massage, then for a consultation with her style guru. I got to go on the school run with Gabi, dropping the Brat off at school and Izzie at nursery.

'Duck down. Don't let my friends see you,' Bryony instructed as we approached the school gates. 'I'm pretending you've gone back home to Birmingham!'

I ducked, just for a quiet life. Then at the end of the day I got carted off to the Brat's music lesson.

'Take her with you!' Aunt Lucy screeched at Gabi. 'I told Marcus that I wouldn't be responsible for guarding her and making sure she doesn't run off again!'

'It's not fair!' Bryony whined. 'Why does she have to come with me?'

I went anyway and listened to her playing the flute. Squeak-whistle-whine.

'Now, Bryony, what's the difference between a quaver and a mini-quaver?' her music teacher asked, as if he'd asked her this question a hundred times.

The Brat sealed her lips tight and refused to play another note. Apparently I was putting her off again.

'My friends think you've got stupid hair,'

she told me on the way home. 'They said if they had hair like yours they'd go to the hairdressers and have it all cut off!'

That was Wednesday.

'Still here?' Anna said to me when she arrived on Thursday. 'Did you leave this lid off the Lurpak Lite?'

Aunt Lucy took her to one side and spent half the morning complaining about me.

'You want to come to park with me and Jude?' Gabi asked me in her funny English. Izzie went to nursery three mornings a week, and this was one of them.

Anything to escape from the Dyson demon and the wicked aunt.

'How's your mum?' Joe asked me when he showed up with his kid brother, Leo.

'The same,' I frowned. I hadn't heard since Tuesday, which seemed like a century ago.

Joe said it was tough, I said it wasn't too bad because I was missing exams, which was cool. I don't know who I was trying to kid.

'I hear the Duchess is giving you a hard

time,' he said in a big, stagey whisper, from behind his hand.

'What duchess?'

'Y'know, Lucy-Loo.'

I grinned. 'Who told you?'

Joe nudged Gabi. 'I have my sources.'

Then the Blob fell out of his pushchair and we had to buy him an ice cream to stop him yelling.

That night there was bad news from the hospital.

No, not what you're thinking. But the thing was, the ward where Mum was had developed a virus infection and nobody was allowed in or out. No visitors. No patients to be admitted or sent home.

'I'm in quarantine,' Mum told me.

It was great to hear her voice at least.

'They found this poxy bug on the ward and sealed us off for at least four days. We're being fed off disposable plates with plastic cutlery.'

'That sucks,' I agreed. I told her I'd been to the park, to make her think things were

looking up and to hide my disappointment
that, no matter what happened, I wouldn't
be able to visit her this weekend.

'And then,' she said, saving the big news
till last, 'they've decided I need to have an
op, on Monday.'

'An op?' You know how slowly you take
things in when they're serious. My mind was
clunking along like I was a computer made
in the dark ages – before the year 2000.

'Yeah, an operation to remove part of my
pancreas.'

I sat down on the hall floor, sliding down
the wall and slumping with my legs straight
out. 'God, Mum!'

'Don't worry. I'll be fine. They'll get rid of
the bit that's gone bad and leave me with the
part that still works.'

'Monday?' I echoed. Today was Thursday.
That meant Friday, Saturday, Sunday . . .

'What about Monday?' the Brat interrupted,
seeing me slumped on the floor. She ran off
to fetch Aunt Lucy, who snatched the phone
and quizzed Mum for the info.

'But we can't possibly cancel our trip!' she

stressed. 'It's all paid for and the money's non-refundable.'

I left her to it and limped upstairs holding my stomach. Weird – I felt as if I'd been kicked by a donkey. That's what bad news does to you.

Eight

'Where's Marcus got to?' Aunt Lucy kept looking at her watch. 'It's typical of him to be late back the day before we're due to go on holiday. I sometimes think he does it on purpose.'

Unbelievable – it was still only Thursday. Time seemed to have come to a stop.

'Gabi, did you pack Luke's new swimming trunks? Make sure that Bryony's case will zip up properly, then iron my white linen trousers again. You let creases in them last time.'

Fetch and carry – Gabi was more of a slave than an au pair. She put the Blob to bed at seven but he stayed awake squawking until nine, though Izzie went down like a dream. And still Uncle Marcus wasn't back home with Luke.

'Marcus, where are you?' Aunt Lucy spat into the phone. 'What do you mean, a fatal accident on the motorway, they've blocked off two lanes? Oh dear – at this time, of all times. Couldn't you come off at the next junction and find a different way?'

It was ten-thirty before they finally made it home.

'I'm absolutely exhausted,' my aunt complained. 'We have to be ready by six and at the airport by seven.'

Actually, it was Uncle Marcus who looked worn out. He threw down his car keys and straight away hit the bottle.

'Don't worry, I've packed everything!' Aunt Lucy said sarcastically.

Which was a lie, since she hadn't even seen the inside of a suitcase – it had been Gabi doing the packing, with me secretly lending a hand.

'Can I trust you to remember your own passport?' Aunt Lucy asked him. 'Or shall I keep it safe in my hand luggage?'

The Brain raided the fridge for frozen pizza. He slapped it in the oven. 'Can I bring my laptop on holiday with me?' he asked.

'No. I'm not having you burying your head in your computer instead of enjoying yourself,' my aunt said.

'Sure, why not,' Uncle Marcus contradicted.

No bets taken on whose answer Luke went for.

'And one other thing,' Aunt Lucy went on. 'Your sister rang.'

Uncle Marcus looked over the top of his whisky glass. 'And?'

'She has to have surgery.' The tone of voice was flat, like you might say the pizza was in the oven or the window cleaner had been.

Uncle Marcus nodded. 'At least they're prepared to operate – that's something. If it were hopeless, they wouldn't even bother. When do they plan to do it?'

'Monday. I told Jessica we couldn't possibly put off going to Florida. She understood.'

'You don't think I should stay and you should take the children?' Uncle Marcus hesitated.

Aunt Lucy jumped as if a bee had stung her. 'Don't be absurd, Marcus. What good would that do? No, I told you – Jessica's perfectly OK about us going.'

'Yeah, Dad!' Bryony insisted.

'I'm not going if you don't come,' Luke cut in. 'I want to visit a motor-boat show in Miami. You'll have to drive me down. Can we hire a new Ford Mustang?'

Uncle Marcus half shut his eyes and looked around the kitchen until his gaze rested on me. 'What about Harmony?' he asked, opening them suddenly.

'They've closed the ward. She can't visit until after the operation,' Aunt Lucy said.

'No, I mean, are we taking Harmony with us?' It was obviously the first time he'd noted there might be a problem – like, one inconvenient niece to be accounted for.

Bryony gave a short. 'No way!'

'You mean, take pity on the poor relation?'

Luke scoffed. 'Just hang on a minute, Dad. You've been reading too much Dickens. This is the twenty-first century, not the flipping nineteenth!'

Aunt Lucy folded her arms. 'Marcus, don't even think about it. How could we possibly get Harmony a ticket at this late stage, for a start?'

'I don't want her to come!' the Brat wheedled.

'Pizza!' Luke remembered, diving for the oven. 'Oh no, it's burnt to a cinder!'

'So what?' Uncle Marcus was talking about me, not the Brain's late night snack.

'I told you Harmony would be more trouble than she was worth,' Aunt Lucy reminded him.

Gabi, who had been doing last-minute ironing in the nearby laundry room, suddenly pursed her lips, clanked down the iron and took a pile of clothes upstairs.

'What about *her*, then?' My uncle's brain registered the fact that they had a spare au pair hanging around the place. 'She's not coming with us either, is she?'

Aunt Lucy tutted. I was looking from her to him and back to her again.

'Is she?' Uncle Marcus repeated.

'No, Marcus. As you recall, *we* decided to give Gabi the week off provided that she stays here to keep an eye on the house for us.'

He nodded. 'Problem solved then. We have a built-in babysitter at no extra cost. Harmony stays right where she is with Gabi.'

As he said – problem solved! He wasn't going to worry about Gabi's week off.

But it did suit me to be offloaded, thank you very much. And it was definitely what Luke, Bryony and my lovely Aunt Lucy wanted to happen, as you already know.

They were *leavin', leavin' on a jet plane, didn't care when they'd be back again, oh-oh, I hated to see them go-o!* Not!

Gabi and I drove Izzie and Jude to the airport in the BMW, while the others went in a taxi. I had the words of an old song ringing in my head. *Leavin' on a jet plane* . . .

. . . With six pieces of luggage for the hold

and four carry-on items, not including the Brain's laptop. They went first class so they didn't have to queue at the check-in desk.

'It's OK, darling. Daddy's firm is paying for it,' Aunt Lucy told Luke. As if he was worried.

'She didn't wear her dress!' Bryony hissed, telling her last tale on me before she left. 'She's in her horrid baggy trousers and trainers.'

'I know, dear. But there's nobody around to see.'

'I'm going to pretend she's Gabi's sister and nothing to do with our family!' the Brat decided.

Like I said, it's hard to believe that a kid could be *so* mean, but she's only eight and Mum's right – it's the way they've brought her up.

Gabi carried Jude to the passport check, while I held Izzie's hand. Announcements came over the intercom, flight and gate numbers flashed up on the Departures screen.

'Pushchair,' Aunt Lucy demanded when it

came time for Gabi to hand Jude over. The baby was dumped in his chair, while Izzie kept tight hold of me.

'You have a good time,' Gabi told her, crouching down and giving her a hug. 'You say big hi to Mickey Mouse!'

Uncle Marcus's phone was ringing as they showed their passports and tickets. 'No, Tom, I can't take any calls for the next few hours. I'll be over the Atlantic, for chrissakes!'

They were through passport control and I was heaving a giant sigh of relief until, at the last second, Aunt Lucy turned to face Gabi and me.

'Don't contact us unless there's an emergency,' she warned Gabi. 'If I don't hear from you about Jessica's op, I'll assume that no news is good news.'

Gabi nodded slowly, watching the little ones go with a tear in her eye.

'And don't let Harmony out of your sight, remember. She's run away once and might do it a second time, knowing her.'

Gabi nodded again. Next to Aunt Lucy she

looked young and fresh and natural. Slim, not stick-thin. Alive.

Ah, yeah – that was why Aunt Lucy treated her so mean!

'Anna will be in later today, and again on Monday,' she reminded Gabi, as if she wasn't capable of keeping me in check by herself.

'Goodbye. Have cool time,' Gabi said. Izzie was starting to blub and Jude was wriggling in his chair. 'Let's go, 'Armony.'

So we went. The rich Harrises jetted off, leaving the poor relation to mope among the ashes.

Nine

Anna has to stack the dishwasher in a special way. If a single knife is out of place, or a cup the wrong way up, she has to take everything out and start again. And she won't let anyone else press the buttons.

'Did Mr and Mrs Harris get off OK?' she asked Gabi as she waged war on the crumbs lurking under the bread board.

'Fine,' Gabi told her. Without the Blob glued to her hip she looked uncomfortable and out of place.

Wipe-swish-scrub. Anna banished the crumbs with her damp cloth. 'That must be the service engineer for the security system,' she said when the side doorbell rang, dashing off on her scrum-half legs to answer it.

'Phew!' Gabi sat down at the kitchen table.

'I like your top – it's cool,' I said. Floaty fabric, two layers – the bottom one was white and the top one was printed with big pink roses.

'It's from Coast. Joe bought it for my birthday.'

'Cool.' I sat down opposite her. 'When was your birthday?'

'Last month. Joe and me had been seeing each other for two days and he bought me present.'

'He's cool,' I murmured.

Gabi nodded and smiled.

'The main control panel is in here, beside the wall unit.' Anna swept back in with the engineer, swooshing Gabi and me out of the kitchen with a filthy look.

'That woman!' Gabi said, with a shake of her head.

We made our way upstairs to Gabi's room, and she invited me in.

It was the first time I'd seen the au pair's

quarters – no TV, no built-in hair-dryer here. The room was poky and overlooking the garage.

'Yeah, what's her problem?' I said, plonking down on the single bed, where I could find room between Gabi's jeans and tops and make-up. Suddenly I was feeling more at home.

'Life! Life is Anna's problem!' Gabi laughed. 'You like this music?' She handed me a CD and told me to stick it on the player. 'I have surprise.'

'Who for?'

'For you.'

Footsteps along the landing made us stop talking and listen to Anna telling the alarm man where the sensors were. 'There's one over the arched window there, and one in every bedroom. They all have to be checked . . .'

'A surprise for me?' I quizzed after the footsteps had faded. 'It's not my birthday or anything.'

'You have hard time,' Gabi said in a low voice. 'I watch, I listen.'

'Oh yeah, that.' A hard time with my mum. An even harder time with Aunt Lucy.

'At home in Romania I have three brothers and two sisters. We fight, we argue. My big brother, Valentin, he tells me what to do, who to see, what skirt not to wear. I answer back. My little sisters borrows my clotheses . . .'

'Cool,' I nodded. I didn't have a clue where Romania was, but I knew I'd like it.

'At home in Romania we have small house. I want to be student, but there is no money. I work here, save for college, learn to be photographer.'

I felt another 'Cool' coming on and let it out, even though I was sounding boring.

'Your mother, what does she do?' Gabi asked.

I told her.

'Good!' Gabi grinned. 'Actress is nice work.'

'About this surprise,' I reminded her.

Gabi went to the door and made sure Anna wasn't around. 'You pack bag,' she whispered. 'We meet Joe in park in half an hour.'

'What d'you mean, pack my bag?' Doh! I managed to sound mega dumb.

'T-shirts and stuff. Not too much.'

'Why? Where are we going? What's Joe got to do with it?'

'Surprise!' Gabi insisted, dragging me off the bed and shoving me out of the door. 'I come to your room in thirty minutes, OK!'

I turned and gawped at her. 'We're not going to Romania, are we?'

She laughed. 'No. In Romania we meet Count Dracula! Where we go is not so scary!'

'Where then?' I heard Anna downstairs checking sensors and giving orders. 'Where?' I hissed.

'Sshh!' Gabi knocked gently and came into my room.

I'd packed my mini rucksack, but was still worrying over my swimming cossie. 'Shall I bring this?'

She nodded and tiptoed to the window to look out at the park. 'Joe is there already!' I joined her, and sure enough I could see the boyfriend, minus little Leo, waiting by the swings in his sports shades and a white sweatshirt. He saw us at the window and waved his car keys at us.

For a wild sec I was ready and willing to swing out and climb down the ivy like they do in Famous Five books. By this time I'd really got into the spirit of things.

'Is OK, Anna is still with security man,' Gabi assured me. 'Is good that we leave without questions, is all.'

So we didn't overdo things in the Enid Blyton department – we went quietly downstairs and out the normal way through the front door, down the white steps and on to the busy pavement. Joe had come to the park gate and we could see him grinning at us.

'But where are we going?' I asked as we crossed the road.

Joe hurried us around the Square to his car. 'Let's go!' he urged. 'We have to leave now if we want to beat the Friday rush hour at the other end.'

My head was buzzing with questions, but I was getting no answers. I got in the back of the tiny green Citroen and strapped myself in.

'M25, here we come!' Joe announced, turning the ignition. 'What's the latest we can get back?'

'Early Monday,' Gabi answered. 'Before Anna comes to clean.'

'What did you tell her about today?'

My ears were pricked up in the back seat like a curious bunny rabbit, I can tell you.

'I tell lie. I said me and Harmony were going to Tate Modern. Anna said OK, but don't let her out of my sight!'

'Nice one.' Joe eased into the traffic, phut-phut. His car probably had about half a cylinder and a sewing-machine engine.

'Hey guys, where are we going?' I yelled above the whine. M25 didn't give me any real clues.

'Wait and see,' Gabi told me all the way out to the ring road and the motorway.

Joe took the Dartford Tunnel exit, into open countryside with fields and cows.

'Where – are – we – going?' I asked for the hundredth time. We were heading south. It was two in the afternoon. The sun was shining.

At last Gabi dug into her bag and pulled out a fistful of tickets. She turned and waved them in my face.

And, I'm not kidding, it was like 'Cinderella, you *shall* go to the ball!'

I was on this ferry. The wind and spray blew in my face. Wow! I mean, wow!!

This was Gabi and Joe's surprise. The tickets had said 'EuroDisney' in big letters. That's EuroDisney, as in Paris, France.

Gabi said if the Harrises wouldn't let me join in their fun, then she, Gabi Petrangiu and her boyfriend, Joe Taylor, would do something about it. 'We already planning to go to EuroDisney, and we want you to come too! We got special last-minute deal! We have cool time!' she promised. 'Mickey Mouse, Pocahontas, Winnie Pooh!'

'I've never been to Disney,' Joe told me. 'This is gonna be awesome!'

So we arrived in Dover and the little Citroen phut-phutted up the ramp on to this massive ferry. Then we dumped the car and climbed some narrow metal steps on to the passenger deck. Joe queued for euros while Gabi and I worked out where the bars and restaurants were.

'Watch it!' an old man said.

I'd barged into him when the boat rocked to one side. 'Sorry!' I muttered. *Not!*

'Kids!' he mumbled.

We staggered on past a choccy machine, a self-service café selling croissants, up to the blunt end of the ferry, where we stepped out on deck. There were the cliffs in the distance, a wide trail of foam in our wake. *Goodbye, England!* Then we trotted round to the pointed end where there was nothing but brown sea ahead of us. I'd like to have said 'blue sea' – you know, clear and sparkling. But no, it was sludge brown, and that's the truth.

'Cool,' Gabi said, standing there with the wind in her hair, like the main woman in *Titanic*.

'Very cool,' I agreed. The wind had this effect of whipping away all my worries, leaving my mind fresh. I won't say I'd forgotten about Mum and her operation exactly, but it wasn't cluttering up my every waking moment. Is that mean and shallow of me? Anyway, the wind zinged against my cheeks and the world opened up.

'I got the dosh,' Joe said, coming up behind us and putting his arm around Gabi's waist. 'I already booked the hotel on the Net. Everything's fixed up in advance. All we have to do is sit back and relax.'

I reckon my eyes were sparkling, and I must have had the biggest stupid grin on my face. 'Pinch me!' I begged. 'Tell me I'm not dreaming!'

Ten

The Magic is closer than you think!

That's the EuroDisney spin, and wow, was it true! I was dreaming with my eyes wide open, being met and greeted by Minnie Mouse, stepping down Main Street, yee-haaahing in Frontierland in my cowboy hat, getting sprinkled with Tinker Bell's dust. You name it, I was in there doing it.

'Me Tarzan, you Jane!' One second I'm deep in the heart of the jungle under an umbrella of trees. A man with muscles and a loincloth is swinging on a creeper towards me.

Next, I'm sitting in a cart, being chased at top speed through a deep, dark mine, racing by ancient stone statues in Indiana Jones's Temple of Doom. Sca-ary!

Then, before I've even recovered from that, a Dwarf slaps a floppy felt hat on my head and drags me into a cottage to have tea with Snow White.

'Whoah! Hang on justy a doggone minute. I'm eleven – way too old for this!' I cry.

And Joe leaps in to rescue me.

He and Gabi whisk me off to munch burgers served by a waitress on roller skates. Wicked!

Afterwards, I just happen to be wearing Mickey Mouse ears (OK, so I'm eleven, so what?) and chatting to Pinocchio when a couple of chipmunks wander up and take me off to a bandit shoot-out.

I kid you not. I could also have flown on a magic carpet and shaken hands with Captain Hook (ouch!) if I'd had time.

Oh, and the hotel that Joe had booked us into. Think wooden boardwalks and a sheriff's office. Think forts and teepees. Yee-hah!

'Waaall, Aah guess Aah'll mosey on down

to the old saloon!' Joe had said in the worst fake-cowboy accent you ever heard, before he stepped out for a beer.

It was our first night in the hotel, before we'd really seen any sights or lived the dream.

That left Gabi and me to experience the wonder of our Wild West room.

'You wanna watch TV or listen to music?' Gabi asked.

'Music,' I said. Which meant we could chat better. 'Thanks,' I began.

'For what?' Gabi settled back on her bed, arms behind her head, wiggling her bare toes.

'For all this.' *For lifting me out of my misery and treating me like I was someone, not just dirt under people's feet.*

'Thank Joe. He fixed it.'

'Yeah, but I bet it was your idea.'

'Maybe. Listen, 'Armony, I don't like to say this because Mrs Harris – she's my boss, but the way that woman treats you is bad news.'

'You too,' I pointed out. 'OK, so she is your boss, and she pays you, but not nearly enough!' Aunt Lucy never heard of the Minimum Wage, I bet. She's still in the era of slave labour – 'Work your fingers to the bone, and if you're clapped out, then off with your head!'

Gabi smiled. 'Look at it this way – if Mrs Harris didn't give me job, I don't take Baby Jude to park and I don't meet Joe, so I don't never fall in love.'

I thought this one through. 'Y'mean, it's kind of Fate?'

She nodded, then turned the talk back to me.

'But your problem is more bad. I mean, Mrs Harris is Family!' (With a capital 'F', the way Gabi said it.)

'Yeah, I'm stuck with her,' I agreed bluntly.

'But Family should love one another. Family means being there to help always!'

I sighed. 'In Romania maybe. But this is England, and it's every man for himself.' Which makes me sound like an eleven-year-old who's been round the block a few times, and that was the way I was feeling right then, I can tell you.

'Hey, 'Armony, you like this song?' Gabi changed the subject, jumping up from the bed and beginning to dance.

I joined in. 'Yeah,' I grinned.

Then, ''Armony, you wanna come for a swim?' she asked.

'Nah.'

'Why not?'

I dug out my cossie and showed her. 'Because.'

'Yeah,' she admitted after she'd seen the frogs. And she dropped the idea. 'This is fun,' she murmured, flicking channels with the volume turned down. 'I hope Izzie and Baby Jude, they have fun too.'

She was missing them, which shows what a nice person Gabi is.

We talked about Romania again. Then about Joe. He came back in as Gabi told me about his legs. 'Legs is important,' she confided, with her back to the door so she didn't see him open it. 'Back 'ome in New Zealand, Joe goes surfing. He has nice legs.'

'Jeez, my ears are burning!' he muttered.

'Girls, come down and grab a barbie before you starve to death.'

Then it was more yee-haahing and banjo music:

'You're mah sun, mah stars up in the sky,

Chantelle baby, Aah'll lurve youuu till Aah die!'

. . . then lots of yawning after a long, mind-blowing day, then bed.

I've already told you about Saturday *day*.

Honestly, I felt as if I didn't have a care in the world, and I was liking Joe and Gabi more and more. In my mind I was planning the perfect wedding for them – Gabi in a pure white dress carrying starburst lilies. Her shoes would be white high-heeled slingbacks with really pointed toes and a pattern of silvery sequins like ones I'd seen in Faith. It must have been the Disney thing that was making me get carried away like this.

'What haven't we done yet? Where haven't we been?' Joe was asking as we sat down by a chuck wagon. And yeah, he was wearing shorts because the sun was shining, and he had nice legs. It was about four o'clock on Saturday afternoon.

Gabi had dashed up to the hotel room to go to the loo.

'I know, let's take a ride on the Rock 'N' Roller Coaster!'

The phone inside Gabi's bag started ringing, so I rummaged and found it. I knew she wouldn't mind.

'Hello?' I said.

'This sounds cool,' Joe insisted. '0 to 60 in 3 seconds. Crazy!'

'Gabi?' a voice on the end of the phone demanded.

I dropped it like it had given me an electric shock. The clunk of it falling must have switched it off.

Then it rang again, and this time Joe took it. 'Hi, who's that?'

I could tell by his face that it was Aunt Lucy again.

Yeah, that *Aunt Lucy. The wicked aunt.*

Joe held the phone away from his ear as Aunt Lucy launched into whatever it was she'd rung to say. When he saw Gabi coming back out of the hotel, he pointed two fingers to his temple as if he was about to shoot himself in the head.

'Who is it?' Gabi hissed.

'Aunt Lucy!' I warned.

She grabbed the phone from Joe, and I felt my Disney world crumble even as she held it to her ear.

When Gabi came off the phone she was deadly pale.

'She says we has to take 'Armony home on next ferry,' she told Joe in a faint voice.

'Hey,' he answered, 'didn't you tell her she can go take a running jump?' It was the first time I'd seen him without a smile.

Gabi took a deep breath. 'Anna called them in Orlando. She says we snatch 'Armony without asking. She says to Mrs Harris we kidnap her niece.'

'Crazy woman!' Joe grunted.

I felt my stomach turn itself inside out.

'Anna even found out where we come,' Gabi explained. 'She listen at door when I speak on phone to you, Joe. She hear me say

EuroDisney. She act like secret police!'

'She's mad. We don't have to take that kind of garbage!'

If only we could shrug it off as easy as that, I thought. I knew we couldn't though.

Gabi shook her head. 'Mrs Harris is serious. She says we break law, you and me. She talks about calling police if we don't take 'Armony home.'

'Tomorrow,' Joe insisted. 'Listen, we're not doing anything wrong. All we did is give Harmony a break, poor kid.'

'She says we go to jail.'

Poor Gabi, I thought. This is how a dream comes crashing down.

Joe paced up and down by the chuck wagon. 'We're not kidnappers, for chrissakes!'

'That's right, no way!' I agreed. I would stick up for them, say I'd wanted to come to Paris. It had been the most mega surprise of my entire life.

I would badmouth my aunt and tell everyone about the lousy way she and the Brain and the Brat had treated me, no problem. Only there was no actual law against being bitchy and mean, I realized. And in the back of my mind I had a sneaky suspicion that maybe – just maybe – someone like Aunt Lucy could persuade a court of law that Joe and Gabi really had abducted me. My head was reeling big time.

'If we take 'Armony back tonight we don't go to jail,' Gabi explained.

'Of all the mean-minded so-and-sos . . . !' Joe ran out of words. *Poor Joe.*

'She's serious.' Gabi could hardly talk. She kept drawing deep breaths and twisting her fingers.

They swung round to look at me.

My turn to take a breath. 'When's the next ferry?' I asked.

I should've realized it had been too good to be true.

We packed in a hurry and closed the door on Disney. *Goodbye, Mickey.*

Joe drove back to Calais without saying a word. If he'd spoken it wouldn't have been fit to repeat, I guess.

We caught the ferry home, and it was the middle of the night before we reached London. The streets were crammed with people reeling out of the clubs on to the pavements. One bloke thumped on our car and cursed as we passed.

We made it to Windsor Square with a dent in our bonnet and a sick feeling in our stomachs.

Radar Anna must have heard the Citroen draw up at the gate because, although it was three o'clock in the morning, she came to the doorstep and waited.

Joe got out and held the door open for me and Gabi. 'I'll call you tomorrow,' he promised.

But Gabi shook her head and refused to get out.

'What's the problem?' Joe asked, shooting an angry glance at the traitor in the doorway.

I was shivering on the pavement, waiting for Gabi to come with me.

'Mrs Harris, she say for me not to come inside,' she said in a little, lost voice. 'She take away my job.'

Joe cleared his throat and rubbed his forehead. 'You mean, the nasty old witch sacked you?'

God, no! I closed my eyes.

Anna came down the path and opened the gate.

'Yes, I lose my job!' Gabi confessed, cupping her hands over her face and finally bursting into tears.

Eleven

'I'm staying here at Windsor Square until Mrs Harris returns from America,' Anna informed me.

Anna the Rottweiler, the Holy Housekeeper.

'It means I've had to rearrange all my other commitments,' Prune-Face went on. 'But I did give my word that I wouldn't let anything else happen to spoil Mrs Harris's holiday, and when I promise something I hold to it.'

My control freak sat me down at the kitchen table and shoved a bowl of cornflakes in front of me.

I hadn't slept a wink and probably looked like it. In fact, I'd laid on the bed for five hours in my T-shirt and shorts, staring at the ceiling and trying not to cry. Now the cornflakes tasted like cardboard.

'Go up and take a shower,' Anna ordered when I pushed the bowl away. She has one of those noses with wide nostrils that look like they're always picking up a bad smell. 'And wear the dress that Mrs Harris bought for you.'

No way, José. I stood up, scraped back my chair and wished I'd had toast so I could scatter crumbs all over Anna's immaculate floor.

Stomp-stomp, up the stairs. I turned the shower setting as hot as I could bear, stood under it and cried for about five minutes. The tears mingled with the steam so you wouldn't have been able to tell.

I scrubbed my face with a hard loofah. Gabi had lost her job for chrissakes, and it was down to me!

Sploosh! The water pricked my red skin like sharp needles.

All because Gabi was a nice, kind person, and generous with it – not mean and nasty like Aunt Lucy, the Brat and the Brain. Now Gabi was penniless and wouldn't be able to go to college. Without a job they would most likely send her back to Romania as an illegal immigrant. Joe would never see her again.

She would pine away in her mountain village, where they still had horses and carts – she told me that herself. The old women would watch her and sigh – poor Gabriella had gone to England and fallen in love with a handsome surfer. Theirs had been a fairytale romance. But Fate had dealt them a cruel blow and the lovers had been forced to part. Now Gabi's poor heart was broken.

And Joe? He would jet back to New Zealand. He would sit alone on a beach, his surfboard cast aside, watching the tide come in and out, staring at the white spray and dreaming of Gabi.

Whoosh! I turned off the shower and watched the water swirl down the plughole in an anti-clockwise direction. In New Zealand it went clockwise, Joe said.

Or is it the other way round? I forget.

Stepping out of the shower, I grabbed a towel.

Just in time – Anna appeared at my door and came in without knocking. She held a phone towards me. 'Mrs Harris wants to speak to you,' she barked.

I clutched my towel. My half-digested cornflakes churned like liquid cement.

'Harmony, you are not – I repeat, *not* – to leave the house before we return! Do you hear?' These were my aunt's first words to me after my Disney adventure.

I swallowed hard and nodded.

'Answer me.'

'Yes.' My voice came out flat as a robot's.

'Anna is under strict instructions not to let you out of her sight. Is that clear?'

'Yes.'

'You are to stay indoors.'

In the background I heard a giggle which sounded suspiciously like the Brat. I could picture her smirking big time as my aunt went off on one.

'I've already told Marcus that once we get

back home I want nothing more to do with his side of the family.'

Fine by me, kiddo!

'For as long as Marcus and I have been married, you and your mother have been nothing but trouble . . .'

Blah-blah! I caught the sound of a band oompahing, which meant the Harrises were probably in the middle of a big Disney parade. Then Luke's voice interrupted his mum. 'Let me talk to her,' he demanded.

Oompah-oompah, one-two, one-two, quick march!

'Sounds like someone's in big trouble,' the Brain began.

What could I say?

'Are you still there, or did you just throw your dummy out of the pram?'

'Ha ha, very funny!' I scoffed.

'Luke, don't waste my credit,' Aunt Lucy warned in the background.

'Listen Harmony, you're lucky Mummy didn't throw you out here and now,' he went on, snidey-snide. 'After what you did, sneaking off and all.'

'We didn't sneak off,' I argued, glaring at Anna the spy. 'Gabi's boyfriend organized the whole thing. No one tried to keep it a secret.' Which wasn't 100 per cent true, I know.

'Yeah well, no doubt you were both sponging off the boyfriend. I expect he paid.'

The band played, oompah-oompah.

'Like you sponge off your dad,' I pointed out. 'And Orlando costs a lot more than EuroDisney.'

'You can't sponge off your own father, stupid.'

'Yeah Luke, I'm the dim one, I know. Just the poor Brummy relation.'

'You said it,' he shot back at me. 'So, what you gonna do now?'

'What d'you mean, what am I gonna do?'

He tutted. 'Figure it out, why don't you? A) Your mum's in hospital. B) She needs an operation. C) She might not pull through. Didn't that enter your thick head?'

Ouch! Ouch-ouch! I threw the phone against the wall, that last-but-one comment hurt so much.

Crunch! Thud! The phone lay lifeless on the cream carpet.

'Stop!' Anna cried, too late. She went down on her hands and knees to pick up the pieces.

I ran out of the room, along the corridor and locked myself in Gabi's old room. I was shaking when I sat down on the narrow single bed.

She might not pull through. The words rattled round inside my head. 'She will!' I told myself over and over. 'Mum's tough. She can beat this, Luke Harris – just you wait and see!'

Anna spent the whole morning banging on Gabi's door. 'Come out!' she growled.

'Make me!'

'Come out, or . . .'

'Or what?' I knew there was no threat Anna could snarl that would make things worse than they already were.

So I sat and looked at the photos in the frames on Gabi's bedside table. There was one of a big family group standing under the shade of a gnarled tree, their arms around each others' shoulders, another of a very old woman, a third of Gabi with three smaller girls, probably her sisters.

'If you don't come out, I'll . . .'

'What? Call Aunt Lucy and snitch on me again?' I taunted.

The old lady in the silver frame had long white hair parted down the middle and plaited. The plaits were wrapped over the top of her head. She wore a bright red and yellow flowered shawl.

'I'll bring someone in to break down the door,' Anna threatened.

'And make a nasty mess? I don't think so!' I laughed.

Then she left me alone for a couple of hours while she did her Dyson Dash. I could hear the machine sucking up dust, even when I opened the little window and leaned out.

She might not pull through!

I shivered and glanced down at myself. I was still wrapped in the towel, with goose-pimples covering my arms and shoulders, so I looked around for something I could put on.

There was just one set of drawers in Gabi's room. I opened the top one and found bras and knickers. The second held Gabi's T-shirts and tops, the third a few pairs of trousers, and the bottom one a couple of winter sweaters. Sooner or later someone would have to pack these and send them to her, wherever she was. Plus the family snapshots. Or else Aunt Lucy would just chuck the lot into a black bag and dump them in the bin, knowing her.

I pulled out a long-sleeved, pink top and put it on. OK, so it was too big, but not that much. I rolled up the sleeves, then tried on a pair of cut-off jeans. They were mega loose around the waist, but I found a belt, put it through the loops and fastened it in the tightest hole. At least now I would stop shivering.

Or so I thought. But actually it was fear that was making me shake, not the cold.

She might not pull through.

In twenty-four hours Mum would be

having an operation to save her life. I pictured nurses lifting her on to a trolley and wheeling her out of the ward. Along corridors, into a lift, then down more corridors to the doors of the operating theatre. A doctor in a mask would give her a needle and she would pass out. They would wheel her through, unconscious. Maybe the last thing she would ever see in this world would be the man in the mask and the needle hovering above her.

She might not pull through.

'Harmony Harris, it's lunchtime. Come out of there!' Anna screeched.

But I wouldn't. I wouldn't eat or sleep until Mum had had her op.

How can you eat when your mum's life hangs on a thread and you can't even talk to her or go to see her?

My lovely mum with her wild red hair and slow, kind voice. 'Come on, kitty-kitty! Thou knowest I love thee more than life!'

And Ophelia would wrap herself around Mum's legs, purring and rubbing, her tail high, her grey head tilted back.

I sat on Gabi's bed with my head in my hands, listening to the tick of the clock downstairs in the hall.

The moment came when I couldn't sit any longer. I think it was about two o'clock and I could hear Anna banging about in the yard below. She must have been emptying the contents of the Dyson, from the sound of the bin lid clattering.

And an idea struck me like a ton of bricks – I didn't have to stay here if I didn't want to! I lay back on the bed with shock, then sat bolt upright.

OK, I know what you're thinking – *She's gonna run away again. She tried that once already and look what happened!*

That's true, I did. And I made a right mess of it, I admit.

But I was an amateur then. It was my very first attempt and I didn't have a clue.

This time, it would be different.

First of all, I make a good plan with no loopholes.

I need money, for a start. Maybe Gabi's got a stash in one of her drawers. This won't be stealing, since I will pay it back as soon as I can.

Yes – there's three twenties and two tens in the top drawer, under the undies. I fold it up and stuff it in my pocket.

Then I need shoes for my bare feet. There's a pair of trainers under the bed. They're two sizes too big, but I fasten the Velcro tight and they stay on my feet – just. What else? I'd better tie a sweater around my waist in case it gets cold later tonight. I could do with a phone, I realize. Is it worth sneaking out when Anna's not looking and grabbing my rucksack from my own bedroom?

No. That woman's got an in-built early warning system. A spider tiptoes across the carpet and she knows about it. Too much of a risk even to try. I'll have to do without my phone.

So how do I escape from Harris Palace, I hear you ask.

I'm coming to that.

You remember the little window? It overlooks the garage, like I said earlier. If you open it fully, there's just enough room to squeeze through. This brings you out on to a sloping roof. You need guts, but you can creep along the roof, crabwise, not looking down, until you come to an edge overlooking the garage doors.

Ah, but that's no good, because the gates leading out of that small courtyard are automatic – you need a remote control to open them, and they're too high to climb. Anyhow, you'd probably set off an alarm.

This is what I mean about planning things properly. Don't try something that you know is not going to work.

OK, so you're out on the sloping roof and you choose another direction. This way takes you over the ridge of the roof and down the far side. Imagine the garage sticking out of the side of the main house. To the front is the courtyard leading to the big double gates, but to the back there's just a garden below you, with a much lower wall at the far edge of it. Plenty of bushes and trees to keep you hidden when you leap down from the low roof.

I know this because I see them when I peer down, and I catch my hair in a twig when I jump. The leaves rustle and the twig snaps. I swear under my breath and weave between the shrubs.

She might not pull through.

I hate you, Luke Harris, for saying that!

I crouch down to catch my breath, glancing back at the house, thinking they should have alarmed the window to the au pair's room, the cheapskates! The house looks tall and empty – a miserable place.

Now it just takes one last effort to climb the garden wall and jump down into a back street.

Oof! I breathe out as I land on the smooth stone setts and check both ways. The street is empty. I'm free.

Twelve

I'm free and I'm heading for the Queen Elizabeth Hospital, Edgbaston.

First thing, I have to find a phone booth that works.

Flap-flap – my too-big trainers slap the pavement as I scoot along Windsor Square, across the park to a more main road at the far side. I've seen phone booths there when I've been playing with Izzie and Leo.

I'm not looking back, and I'm not thinking about Anna and what she'll do when she finds I've escaped.

The back of the booths are papered from ceiling to floor in nasty business cards and fly-posters. Two phones are for cards-only, but the third takes coins.

Jeez, I don't have any coins! Only three twenties and two tens. I nip into a shop and buy a bottle of water, get the change and bring it back to the phone booth. The phone's now in use.

Four girls about my age are walking my way, carrying school bags and talking in loud voices.

'Which railway station do trains for Birmingham leave from?' I ask them on the off-chance, which is what I was going to find out on the phone from Ticket Information. The girls stare at my too-big trainers and clothes and reckon I'm some sort of weirdo. 'Why d'you wanna know?' one asks. They're stopping and gathering round, ready to give me a hard time.

''Cos my mum's sick and I have to get to the hospital.' I come out with it to strangers, just like that.

Which makes them look at me even more weirdly. 'Try Euston,' one of the others suggests, pulling her mates away. *Leave her – she's a nutter!*

They go on down the street, looking over their shoulders and giggling.

Euston?

Do I trust them? What if they're having me on?

'Euston,' a woman by the phone booth confirms. She's heard the whole thing while she sits on her sleeping-bag and begs. She's about forty, with dyed blonde hair where the roots are left dark. She's wearing a dirty, black padded jacket zipped up to her chin, even though it's summer. She doesn't have a dog to help her cadge dosh.

'Euston,' she says again.

That's good enough for me. I nod at her, give her fifty pence and head for the nearest tube station – a few hundred metres down the main road. I find the map and work out the route to Euston – pretty easy, actually. Listen, this is the second time I've done this, OK.

But I'm not happy down here in the crush again, buying my ticket, squeezing through barriers, riding the escalators. I feel hemmed in and I don't want to breathe the stale air.

People don't make eye contact – this is a mega rule that you don't break. If you do you'll probably be struck dead. Anyway, they just shuffle past you, looking at their feet. No smiles, no friendliness.

But I make it on to the train. I'm stressed out now – am I going in the right direction? Will I miss my stop? I keep an eye on the map above the seats and try not to mind the fat woman with three shopping bags who stands on my toes.

Euston comes up before I know it. The train slows and stops, the doors slide open. I have to push past the woman with the bags. The door swishes shut as soon as I've stepped down on to the platform. Mind the gap.

Euston. Way Out. Arrows. Exit.

Up the escalator, following the signs to the mainline station.

Now I need a ticket to Birmingham. I have to queue and I'm feeling like I just want to lie down and go to sleep.

She might not pull through. The voice is quieter now, but it's still there.

'Birmingham,' I say to the man behind the glass screen, clutching my money.

'Single or return? How many are travelling?' He gives me a sharp look when I say I'm by myself.

But I grab the ticket and leave. A big electronic screen tells me I have to wait half an hour for the next train, which is due to depart from Platform 3 at 4.28.

I'm on a huge concourse filled with men and women in suits carrying laptops, students with rucksacks, shoppers and tourists. There are more beggars, a juggler and a couple of buskers. Thirty minutes begins to seem like thirty days.

'The next train to arrive at Platform 3 is the 4.28 to Birmingham New Street.' The muffled announcement comes at last.

Weird – yesterday at this time I was yee-haahing with Joe and Gabi in a Wild West saloon. Then this big hand comes along and grabs you, swings you around for a bit and dumps you somewhere else, in another life, another world. That's how it feels – like a giant hand dropping you from a great height.

I'm on the train. We slide over the tracks, clickety-clack. A trolley passes slowly with tea and coffee. I'm hungry but I can't eat. I swig water from the bottle I bought earlier. It's all I'm carrying with me.

This is a high-speed train. It carries me like an arrow to my mum lying in the Q.E. There are long streaks of rain on the window, black and white cows are sitting down in fields. I look at the sky and see that it's full of thunder clouds.

Clickety-clack. Clickety-clack.

'The next stop is Birmingham New Street. This train terminates here.'

I have zilch belongings to make sure I take with me, so I'm ready and waiting at the door when we draw into the station. I press the green button. Ping!

I'm on the platform and sprinting towards the exit barrier, flap-flap. A mini-train carrying parcels and letters heads slowly towards me. I swerve. Then I'm taking stairs two at a time, following arrows to the main exit, breathing hard now. It's not like I'm being chased, but something is pushing me on and making me panic.

Fear again, I reckon.

By now it's pouring down. I see a massive queue for taxis, the rain coming down in torrents in the world beyond the station canopy.

Now, big question – am I gonna find a bus that will take me straight to the hospital, or am I going home to Norma Street?

Think, Harmony! Calm down and catch your breath.

If you go to the Queen Elizabeth, they're not gonna let you in to see your mum. There's an infection on the ward, remember.

Yeah, but I've come all this way! I've escaped from Captain Kleen so that I could see Mum before her op!

They won't let you in this late in the day.

I need to see her.

What for?

To . . . see her. To tell her I love her.

She knows.

To hold her hand, to say everything's gonna be fine.

You don't know that for sure. Wait. Wait until tomorrow.

I go out into the rain.

I take the number 45 bus and head for Norma Street.

When I did calm down, I realized that I didn't even have a key. Great!

Ruth had given it to Ian so he could get in and feed the cat. Ian lives next door and he had the key to my own house.

Get this – I was sitting on a bus in a thunderstorm without a clue about how I was going to get in. You have to admit – my actual escape plan had gone like clockwork, but my long-term strategy left a lot to be desired.

Still, I was back in Brum. The bus took me down Digbeth and out on the Stratford Road. I knew these buildings, these streets. The woman sitting next to me looked at me and smiled sympathetically.

'No coat?' she asked me.

I shook my head, spraying her with raindrops from my wet, rats' tails hair.

I glanced out at fruit and veg stalls, second-hand furniture shops, car showrooms. My watch told me it was ten minutes past seven.

'My daughter's the same – won't wear a coat even if there's a blizzard,' Mrs Chatty informed me. 'I say, you'll catch your death, but she doesn't listen.'

''Scuse me.' I stood up and dripped on her some more. 'This is my stop.'

I got off the bus and stood in the downpour. I was already soaked, so why bother?

No key! The little problem gnawed away at me. Half-seven. Would Ian be in? Should I knock on his door and just ask for the key? Was he dozy enough not to realize that I'd just run away from my rich rellies in London?

Splat-splat – my trainers hit the wet pavement as I trotted past St Michael's towards Norma Street.

No, I'd better not risk calling on Ian. But what then? Still stymied, I wished that I was small enough to crawl in through Ophelia's cat-flap.

Here was my street corner, with its patch of rough grass and rubble where the old swimming-baths used to be. Here was the newspaper shop that sold milk and loo rolls and was open whenever you ran out. I kept my head down and ran on through the rain.

Number 30, where the family with eight kids lived. Number 52, which was empty and boarded up after a fire. Number 60 had new windows and a mega garden with hanging-baskets getting battered by the storm.

Number 64. My little house. It has a black door with a brass letter-box and the original panel of stained glass above it. Ian at number 66 always keeps his blinds down, so there was no risk of him spotting me as I stood like a drowned rat and wondered what to do.

No spare key – that was for sure. Mum says that leaving a key under a stone by the door or on a window sill is like an open invitation to thieves. 'Please come and burgle me!' And no windows open, at least at the front.

Maybe at the back though, which you get to by going to the end of the row, which is number 82, cutting down the side and back along a narrow alley with a high fence to one side. Beyond the fence is a Tesco's car park. Only residents are supposed to use the brick path, which at this time of year was overgrown with dandelions and weeds.

I used it now, to see if there was a way into my house.

Miaow! A black cat crossed my path in the rain. Was that unlucky or lucky? I never remember. I ducked down behind the low wall when I passed the back of number 72, where Ruth and Kelly lived, then straightened up for the final stretch.

But not so fast. I could actually see our back garden when a rickety gate into the alley opened and Ian came out. He spotted me and did a double-take.

'Thought you were in London,' he muttered.

'I was. I came back.' *Doh!*

Ian did his sliding-eyes thing and studied the dandelions. 'Lousy rain.'

'Yeah.' I could see our back door key in his hand. *Gimme, gimme!*

'How's your mum? When's the op?'

'Tomorrow. That's why I came home.'

Long pause. He sniffed and shook rain drops off the end of his nose.

'Are you going to feed Ophelia?' I asked.

A nod. Slidey eyes.

'It's OK, I'll do it,' I zapped in, reaching out for the key. 'Might as well, now I'm here.'

Nod number two.

I took the key. 'Ta.' Then I dashed past Ian into my garden.

Yep, he was that dopey. No, 'Hey, how come you're by yourself?' No, 'Aren't you a bit young to be staying in the house by yourself?' He just handed me the key, turned around and shuffled back into his place.

Rain was coming down so fast that the gutter over our door had overflowed. I had to stand in a waterfall to unlock it.

Click. The lock turned and I was inside at last.

Empty tins of cat food stood in a neat row by the bin. A half-full one stood on the fridge, with a fork and Ophelia's empty bowl. The cold tap dripped into the sink.

'Here, Offie. Here, kitty-kitty!'

No sign of the cat, so I kicked off Gabi's trainers and went upstairs to my room. Off with my wet things and into a dry pair of jeans and a T-shirt. That felt much better – especially after I'd towelled my hair dry.

'Here, kitty! Here, Ophelia!' Downstairs again, I rattled the fork against her dish. Mum's wind-chimes played a light little tune as I brushed against them.

Better water those geraniums, I decided. The soil was bone dry.

I was busy doing this, beginning to breathe normally again and letting something that felt like relief sink in, when the flap clicked and in walked our cat without a drop of rain on her.

I kid you not – she comes in from a thunderstorm, past a leaky gutter and she's dry as a bone. Don't ask me.

'Hey, Ophelia!' I say.

The chimes tinkle, the geraniums drink their water.

'Miaow!' Ophelia says, wrapping herself around my legs and tilting her chin up. This is cat language for 'I'm pleased to see you.' I wasn't Mum, but I would have to do.

I bent down and picked her up, felt her warm, soft fur against my cold cheek.

Thirteen

Ophelia slept on my bed.

And in spite of the fact that Monday was going to be the worst day of my life, I did manage to snooze my way through the night.

I had dreams though.

I was a rock chick in America, doing a big open air concert. I lifted the microphone to my mouth and the words wouldn't come. Major panic. Then I was in a red Ford Mustang trying to overtake thousands of people in a traffic jam to catch up with the guy in the car who knew the words to my song. I never found him.

I woke up, turned over and thumped my pillow into shape, fell into another dream. I was in a park carrying Ophelia. The park had a maze with high hedges and a lake in the middle. I kept meeting people and trying to offload Offie, saying she wasn't my cat. When I reached the lake I threw her in. Ugh!

If I say I woke up even more tired then when I first went to sleep, you'll know why. It was six-thirty when I finally got up and slobbed downstairs. The walls of my stomach were flapping against each other, I was so hungry. So I hit the crisps and biscuits cupboard and snacked on two packs of cheese and onion flavour, my favourites.

Phew, that was better. There was orange juice in the fridge which had passed its sell-by date, but only just. I swigged it, then sat down and considered what to do next.

My situation today had one or two pluses and a squillion minuses.

First plus: I was here.

Second plus: I wasn't at Windsor Square.

Third plus: Anna the Rottweiler couldn't boss me around.

Fourth plus: Ophelia was still pleased to see me when she came downstairs. She did the leg-rubbing thing and gave a purr.

Now for the minuses.

A) Mum still had pancreatitis.

B) *She might not pull through.*

C) Nobody knew I was here, so there wasn't anybody I could ask for help. Not Ruth and Kelly because Ruth was the one who'd dobbed me in last time. Not Ian because he was – well, Ian!

D) I had to get to the hospital.

E) Then I had to smuggle myself into a ward that wasn't letting visitors in.

F) I had to do all this *before* Mum went for her op, and I didn't even know what time that was.

G) God knows what was happening at Windsor Square. Had Anna found out I'd done a runner? Had she contacted Aunt Lucy in Orlando?

H) Gabi had lost her job because of me.

I don't need to go on with this list – it's too depressing.

I thought about scoffing a third packet of crisps but decided against it.

'Miaow!' Ophelia asked for her breakfast.

This brought me round a bit – enough to feed her then go back upstairs and get dressed. Enough to make me decide that there was no point getting swamped by the minuses – much better to count up the remains of Gabi's dosh, and discover that I probably had enough for a taxi to the Q.E.

Mum kept a taxi company's number by the phone. I rang it and ordered one for eight o'clock.

'Name?'

'Harmony Harris.'

'Address?'

'64 Norma Street.' I lowered my voice and tried to sound like I'd been ordering taxis for years.

'I don't think so, love,' the taxi man said, realizing I was under age. 'Try asking your mum to give you a lift to school before you ring us next time.' Click.

Which left me with the number 62 bus option, along with every office worker and shop assistant struggling to get to work in the rain.

Yeah, it was still raining.

Sitting on a steamed-up bus in another traffic jam on the Bristol Road, I looked around at the other passengers. How come they didn't have pancreatitis, I wondered. How come my mum, who definitely didn't deserve to be this ill, got it when she didn't even drink?

I was having a choking, mega 'It's not fair!' moment and nearly missed my stop. I hopped off at the last moment and set off at a jog towards the main entrance to the hospital.

They're scary places, hospitals. Ambulances zoom up with their blue lights flashing. Paramedics in green uniforms jump out, carry patients on stretchers into the Accident and Emergency Department. Doors swish open and swallow them. Outside in the rain, relatives sit on benches and smoke cigarettes. Inside, there are desks, waiting rooms, signs, lifts, corridors . . .

'Which ward do you want?' a chubby man at Reception asked from behind a bank of Get Well flowers waiting to be delivered.

'Nothing. None. I don't!' I yelped, like someone just stood on my toe. I sprinted off to the Ladies' loo.

How come hospital loos are so naff? You think they'd be mega clean and hygienic. But no, they run out of loo paper, and slimy pink liquid-soap blobs down from the dispenser into the sink. I'm needing to pee every five minutes, I'm so scared.

Eventually I creep out of the Ladies' and scoot off down a corridor, trying to look like I know my way.

Uniforms are everywhere. Nurses, doctors, porters.

'What are you up to?' they all seem to be saying, with mean looks through narrow slits of eyes. 'You shouldn't be here – you're a kid!'

Or am I paranoid?

'My mum is sick. She might not pull through!' I want to yell at everyone. But instead I swiftly turn a corner into a new corridor and follow a sign saying 'Radiography'.

'Don't go through there!' a woman warns as I go to push open a heavy door.

I glimpse a massive, shiny machine – the kind they slot people into for body scans on 'ER'.

The staff woman makes a grab for my arm. 'Are you lost?' she quizzes.

I shake my head and give her the slip. Yes, lost! Yes, scared to death and panicking in case my mum doesn't make it. I cut back the way I came.

I turn more corners, avoid crashing into trolleys, try not to stare at the young kid on crutches with only one leg . . . and I come back to Reception, and Mr Chubby Beady Eyes glaring at me from behind the pink carnations.

So I tough it out and march up to the giant notice board, looking for directions to Ward D.

'Infection – Ward closed to all visitors' it says on a temporary red sign. But I'm not going to let that stop me – not now.

''Armony,' somebody said over my right shoulder.

At first I thought it was one of those voices inside my own head.

"Armony!'

I turned and came face to face with Gabi.

'Gabi!'

We stared at each other without saying anything for ages.

'We knew you'd be here.'

We? I looked beyond her and saw Joe watching us. 'What's going on?' I gasped.

'Anna called police,' Gabi told me.

She and Joe had hauled me off to a café behind the main reception.

Press re-wind to yesterday afternoon.

'It seems she panicked,' Joe explained.

I was sitting there with a Coke, not knowing whether to laugh or cry. Anna panicking pushed me towards a giggle-cum-snort.

'By about half-five she thought you'd gone too quiet. She did a bit of hammering on Gabi's door and got no reply, then decided you'd passed out for lack of food or something. She got it into her head that you were lying unconscious.'

Nope. I was climbing out of the window,

scrabbling over the garage roof, waving bye-bye to Harris Palace . . .

'We heard all this when the cops contacted us at about ten o'clock.'

'You're serious? She really did call the police?' I gasped.

'Yeah. They said as far as they were concerned, no crime had been committed, call a handyman to break down the door, and a doctor if she was that worried.'

'Did she contact Aunt Lucy?' I asked. I had one eye on the clock behind the counter, and more than half my mind still on the problem of how I was gonna get to see Mum before her op. But I had to hear Joe and Gabi out.

'No. She doesn't want to spoil holiday,' Gabi told me.

'She went with the handyman option,' Joe explained. 'A guy called Arthur who lives downstairs from Anna in Fulham, apparently. He comes over and breaks down the door – neatly, I guess. Then Anna discovers you're not lying unconscious.'

'I climbed out of the window,' I confessed.

'I couldn't stand it there a minute longer. I had to borrow some of your money, but I'll pay it back as soon as Mum's better.'

Gabi nodded. 'Is OK. First thing Anna thinks is ring me.'

'Why?'

'She thinks Gabi's in on the Great Escape!' Joe laughed in a non-funny way. 'Gabi was with me at my mum's place. Her phone went and Anna kicked off. Gabi had planned to help you run away like she did last time. Didn't Gabi know that it was against the law and this time she was dialling 999?'

I snorted again. 'How am I supposed to have contacted Gabi? I didn't even have my phone. I didn't know where she was!'

'Yeah, well, Anna wasn't listening to reason. She slammed down the phone on Gabi and went ahead and called the police. Next thing we know, there's a knock on our door – they've traced Gabi through me to Mum's address. This woman sergeant wants to know if we know where you are, and do we realize that we could be facing a charge of kidnapping?'

'Luke told me Mum might not pull through,' I said in a small voice, changing the mood completely.

''Armony, don't think that way,' Gabi whispered, putting one hand over mine where it fidgeted on the table.

'We know why you did a runner,' Joe said. 'We explained to the cops as best we could – that your mum was in hospital and that you were worried sick.'

My heart sank when I heard this. I began to look around for blue uniforms amongst the white coats.

'The sergeant asked us all the questions you'd expect, like did you have any money, was this the first time you'd tried to run away, where were you likely to head?'

'We say we know nothing for sure,' Gabi cut in. 'But we give name of hospital.'

Right, my heart was in my boots by this time. 'Did they get in touch with Mum?' I asked. *Please let the answer be no!*

Gabi and Joe shrugged.

'I have to see her!' I said, standing up and pulling my hand free from Gabi's.

"Armony, police are here!' Gabi protested. 'Joe and me, we drive up early this morning to help. We find police – a different one – waiting outside Ward D.'

I sat down again in despair, like someone had punched me and all the air had gone out of my body.

'Come on,' Joe said gently, standing up himself. 'Let's go and face the music.'

Gabi, Joe and I went up in the lift and along the corridor to Mum's ward.

'How did you get here?' Joe asked me, out of interest. When I told him about the train he seemed pretty impressed. 'This kid has guts,' he told Gabi.

I didn't feel like it right then. I was fighting back the tears.

'Here she is,' Gabi told the policeman outside the door, presenting me for inspection.

He checked me out, asked me if I was OK, radioed in to his sergeant to tell him that I'd showed up safe and well. 'The kid's mum is pretty sick,' he explained.

There was a pause while he took advice.

'There are two family friends here with her, willing to look after her – yeah, the couple we interviewed last night. No, not the aunt and uncle. They're out of the country, left the kid with a housekeeper, apparently. That's the one she ran away from. These two seem OK though.'

More listening. I felt about five centimetres tall, being talked about like a piece of lost luggage.

'No, I didn't speak to the mother,' the policeman said into his radio. 'She's too sick.' *She might not pull through!* Hearing someone else say Mum was really ill made Luke's warning more real than ever.

'OK, Sarge, I'll tell them that.' Clicking off his radio, the man turned to Joe and Gabi. 'We're happy for you to keep an eye on her for the time being,' he informed them. I wasn't listening as he went on about where we would be staying and stuff like that.

A stretcher had just been wheeled into the ward by two porters. I had a glimpse through the swinging doors of the nurses' station, people standing about, rows of beds down the room.

'Infection. No Visitors Allowed'. I read the sign on the door.

I knew that stretcher was for my mum, to take her to the operating room. I've seen stuff like this on 'Casualty'. So this was my last chance and I made a dive for the door.

I was through and sprinting towards the nurses' desk. Two nurses were looking up at me, the stretcher had stopped by Mum's bed, they were lifting her on.

One nurse came out from behind the desk. I dodged and ran on, past a breakfast trolley past patients in their beds.

Mum caught sight of me as they laid her on the stretcher and arranged her tubes. I stopped about two metres from her. She was hooked up to a metal stand, she was taped, labelled and punctured by a hundred needles. But she was still Mum.

'Trust you!' she said to me with a calm smile.

I forced myself to grin back.

The nurse came up to talk to the porters,

there was more kerfuffle going on behind me.

'I went to EuroDisney,' I told Mum. Talk about saying what's *not* important!

'Was it good?' she asked. She could only turn her head as they began to wheel her out of the ward.

'Cool,' I nodded, clutching the side of the stretcher and walking with her.

Gabi grabbed hold of me outside the door to the ward. She held my hand.

Mum was wheeled away down the corridor.

'See you later,' she promised.

Fourteen

I'll spare you the gory details and jump to the bit where Aunt Lucy and the Windsor Square tribe jetted back early from the World of Mickey.

I was in the relatives' room at the hospital, doing a pop-trivia crossword, feeling numb. At least they didn't put me in quarantine too – they decided the infection was close enough to being over.

I should've been thinking, 'Wow, it's well cool – Mum made it!' – which she did, after a four-hour op. But instead I was trying to work out Four Down – 'Her on–off marriage keeps us all guessing' – three letters, middle letter 'L'.

I hadn't got to see Mum yet – she had pulled through, but the nurses were still busy with plastic tubes and bleeping monitors in the High Dependency Unit. But they definitely said she'd be OK (I've told you this three times now, just to make sure). Joe and Gabi had breathed a sigh of relief and gone off to get a cup of coffee at last, when in walks my wonderful aunt.

The first words she said were, 'Harmony Harris, I hope you realize you've dragged us all the way back from Florida with your ridiculous melodramatic gesture!'

I looked up to see Uncle Marcus frowning behind her. No sign of the Brain et cetera.

'How come?' I asked. Like, Doh!

'Your running away from Windsor Square,' Aunt Lucy explained. 'Again!'

My turn to frown. 'Sorry,' I mumbled.

'Yes, we were forced to come back early because of you. We've only just stepped off the plane. None of us have had any sleep, and it's cost hundreds of pounds extra to alter our flight!'

'J-Lo.' I cracked the clue and filled in the squares.

'Harmony, are you listening? My poor children have had to sacrifice half of their Disney vacation! Bryony was beside herself – she cried the entire way home!'

I stood up then and turned my back to look out of the window, down five floors at a car park with hundreds of cars.

You know what Aunt Lucy's like by now. You'd expect her to be bad, but not quite this nasty, the unfeeling cow.

My back view seemed to offend her big style. 'And what do we find when we arrive?' she ranted. 'Nothing less than a full-scale police investigation, that's what! I've just been asked lots of stupid questions by some junior officer who seemed to imply that we hadn't made proper arrangements for you to be looked after while we were away. I was so humiliated!'

Cool, I thought. About time.

'I told him that it was your own mother who should be investigated – not us!'

Say that again.

163

'I insisted you were a child who was totally out of control and in need of proper parental guidance. I suggested they bring in the social services.'

'Lucy!' Uncle Marcus stepped in at last. He looked dog-tired – grey in the face, not like a man who'd just lived the Disney dream. 'All this can wait,' he insisted.

It had to anyway, 'cos a nurse came along and told me in a kind voice that I could see my mum now.

The first words Mum said when she came round from the op will stick in my mind for ever.

It was about four in the afternoon. Two nurses flitted about her bed.

'Give her a little while,' one said as she dashed off carrying a steel bowl full of cotton-wool and gunk. 'She might not know you at first.'

Mum was moving her head feebly from side to side and licking her lips. Then she opened her eyes and tried to focus. She saw me sitting beside her.

'Phuh!' she breathed, like she was blowing a stray hair from her mouth.

'Harmony? Wow-oh-wow-oh-wow!'

Not much as first words go, but she knew me all right, and like I say, I'll always remember them.

Mum pulled through. She made it! Four times, just to be totally clear. Phew!

But now I had Aunt Lucy on my back, and this stupid stuff about social services to deal with.

First off, it was a woman called Sue who worked in the hospital welfare office.

'Are you unhappy?' she asked me straight out. She had long, jet-black hair with a centre parting. She was about fifty. We were in her office next to the hospital chapel.

'I was, but I'm not now. Mum's gonna be fine.'

'Why did you run away?'

'I wanted to see her.'

Sue nodded thoughtfully. 'Had anyone been treating you badly? For instance, threatening you in any way?'

'No,' I lied.

'Did anyone help you to leave London?'

'No.' I did that all my myself – just cut loose and ran. Yeah!

'Thank you, Harmony,' Sue said, closing her file and showing me to the door.

I was left hanging, not knowing if I'd given the right answers or not.

Then it was Round Two with the heavy-weight aunt.

It was the day after Mum's op, and me, Gabi and Joe had stayed overnight at Norma Street. I was feeding Ophelia when Aunt Lucy marched in with the Brain and the Brat – no knocking, just swanning in.

Gabi did a double-take, then recovered. 'Hi, Mrs Harris. Hi, Luke, hi, Bryony. You want toast and orange juice?'

'Gabi!' Aunt Lucy gasped.

The Brain gawped at the half-dead geraniums on the window sill, behind our ancient microwave. The Brat had red, puffy eyes from perma-crying.

'Is this crummy hole the place where you

live?' Luke asked in disbelief. I mean – no jacuzzi!

'I might have known you had a hand in all this, Gabi Petrangiu.' Aunt Lucy went straight for the jugular. 'It was obvious that Harmony couldn't have pulled it off alone.'

'I did!' I protested, seeing before Gabi did which way this was going.

'You sure you don't want breakfast?' Gabi asked.

My aunt steamed on. 'Consider yourself sacked,' she told her nanny. 'That means, in plain English, you are currently unemployed. You no longer work for me.'

Typical. Put Aunt Lucy under pressure and she lashes out. Take Gabi – you couldn't get a kinder, more caring person to look after your kids.

'Fine,' Joe said, coming into the kitchen and quickly picking up what was going on. 'No problem, since you already sacked her, in case you forgot!' He stood beside his girlfriend and outstared my aunt, who turned back to me.

'Harmony, Marcus insists that you come

home with us,' she said. 'Your mother will be in hospital for at least three more weeks, waiting for wounds to heal and stitches to be taken out. Meanwhile, you have to stay at Windsor Square.'

It must have been worse than going to the dentist and having teeth pulled out for her to invite me back.

'No way,' I told her. Like absolutely no way!

Fifteen

Mum was weak after the op, but they made her sit up and had her out of bed on Day Two.

'Ouch!' she said, when they eased her legs over the side of the bed. 'Ouch-ouch!'

'Aunt Lucy sacked Gabi – twice!' I told Mum when the physio finally laid off. Then I had to go back to the beginning and explain who Gabi was and why she was out of a job. Mum didn't say much, but she was thinking hard.

Then I sat on the bed and brushed her hair. 'Do I *have* to go back to London?' I asked. I'd been given twenty-four hours to come round to the idea, while Aunt Lucy and Uncle

Marcus stayed in a big hotel in Birmingham city centre. He was on the phone to Tom about Kyoto, which might be on again, not off. She was talking to Sue in the welfare office.

I'd decided not to worry Mum with all that, but I drew the line about going back to lousy Harris Palace.

'Gabi says she'll stay on at Norma Street with me for as long as we need her.'

Mum tilted her head back. 'I can't afford to pay,' she pointed out.

I kept on brushing her shiny hair back from her pale face. 'Gabi won't mind.'

'OK, let me meet her,' Mum decided.

It was a weird job interview – on a hospital bed with Mum doing more physio – ouch, ouch!

Gabi said it was definitely better if I stayed with Mum now – not saying anything bad about Aunt Lucy, because that's not Gabi's style – but just telling Mum that I would be a bag of nerves wondering how she was if I couldn't come and visit her every day.

I was there, listening to Gabi's funny way
of talking.

'Family is the biggest thing,' she told Mum.
'Harmony runs away from a palace to be with
you. Mother – daughter; nothing is better!'

Mum smiled through the pain while the
physio bent her legs towards her chest. 'I
like her,' she told me. 'You two stay at Norma
Street. I'll have a word with Marcus.'

Which was all totally cool, and call me dim,
but I wasn't expecting what came next. I
mean, I'd done the hard bit – got away from
the Rottweiler Anna in Windsor Square and
legged it back home.

And now I'd found a way of staying close
to Mum . . . or so I thought.

'Jessica,' Uncle Marcus began when he came
to visit later that day. He was alone. Mum
sat up in bed in her one and only nightie,
her red hair gleaming, but with dark circles
under her eyes.

'This bit is difficult,' he said, standing
instead of sitting. 'You're my sister after all.'

'Sit down, Marcus,' Mum said. 'It feels like looking up at a black marble pillar!'

He sat. I was on the other side of the bed, watching his face.

'But Lucy is my wife, and I have to support her.'

I was slow this time not to see what was coming like a dirty great juggernaut. I didn't get it until I caught sight of my bootilicious aunt and Sue the Welfare Worker hovering by the nurses' station at the far end of the ward.

'It's your drinking,' Uncle Marcus explained, not able to look up above the level of the pink cotton bedspread. 'That's the bottom line.'

'What drinking?' Mum wasn't expecting it either. It hit her out of the blue – vroom-wroagh!

'Your consumption of alcohol has reached an unacceptable level,' her brother said stiffly. 'I don't know what exactly is your tipple, Jessica – whether it be wine or something stronger – but whatever it is, it's caused you to be seriously ill, as we all now know.'

'No, we don't !' I yelled.

'Hush,' Mum warned. 'I don't drink, Marcus. It's true I've had pancreatitis, but that doesn't mean I'm a drunk!'

'It's your lifestyle,' Uncle Marcus sighed, while Aunt Lucy and Sue advanced. 'Actors are known to need a drop of Dutch courage before they go on stage. And then there's the binge drinking at last night parties, and so on. Alcoholism comes with the territory.'

'I don't drink,' Mum insisted, still quiet and determined.

My uncle gave her a look that said, 'They all say that,' before Sue swept in.

She drew the curtain around Mum's bed – swish-swish! – and guided Aunt Lucy into the private space with us.

We were face to face with the enemy. My aunt's expression was hard, her eyes dark and angry, her make-up like a mask.

I stared at Sue and Uncle Marcus, but there was no help there.

We were trapped, Mum and me.

Sixteen

'This is a serious allegation,' Sue began.
'Harmony, I'm going to have to ask you to
leave us and go and wait in the visitors' room
while we grown-ups try to work things out.'

Yeah – like, adults know so much more
than kids. Like, they always get it right!

'No, I would like Harmony to stay,' Mum
said. She was swinging her legs off the bed
and trying to stand up. I helped her.

It felt better when she was upright – taller
than Aunt Lucy, on a level with Uncle
Marcus.

Sue Welfare tried to back off then. 'Perhaps
we should postpone this until you're feeling
stronger, Ms Harris.'

'No, we'll sort it now.'

Mum looked like a warrior from *Lord of the Rings*, with her red hair streaming. Amazing.

'No one accuses me without me having my say. I'm supposed to be a drinker, am I? An unfit mother – is that what you're saying?'

'Jessica, please!' Uncle Marcus went several shades paler. 'Don't make a scene.'

Mum took a deep breath. 'You're trying to take my daughter away, and you tell me not to make a *scene*, as you call it. Tell me, Marcus when would it be appropriate to raise your voice above its boring monotone? When the stock market crashes, perhaps?'

'There's no need to be nasty,' Aunt Lucy objected.

Big mistake! She should have kept her head well down.

Mum turned towards her. 'Talking of nasty,' she began.

'Ms Harris – Jessica,' Sue pleaded.

Mum swatted her away and concentrated on Aunt Lucy. 'Harmony ran away from your house, remember! I don't know how you did it, but you actually managed to alienate one of the easiest-going, most good-natured kids around!'

Easy-going. Good-natured. That was me! Yeah!

Mum was on a roll. 'What exactly did you do to make my daughter hate you, Lucy?'

'Nothing,' my wicked aunt muttered. The tan looked yellow, the fingernails were like red claws.

'She refuses to go back and stay with you – there must be a pretty good reason!'

'No. We gave her everything she could possibly want!'

'Except a scrap of human kindness,' Mum snorted. 'Y'know – k-i-n-d-ness! Being warm and welcoming, asking if she was OK every now and then.'

Wow, Mum! She was going in for the kill – no raised voice or waving her hands in the air though.

'Jessica, stop trying to turn this around,' Aunt Lucy protested. 'Sue is here to discuss your drink problem.'

Big pause. Deep breath. 'Go to hell, Lucy,' Mum said.

I was dead proud of her.

Then a nurse popped her head through the gap in the curtains. 'Is everything OK?' she asked.

Mum grabbed the moment. 'Find my medical notes. Get the consultant to come and tell this madwoman, my sister-in-law, that I am not – repeat *not* – an alcoholic!'

It was too much for Aunt Lucy. She turned into a pathetic wimp the moment someone stood up to her.

'Forget it!' she snapped.

'Yes, like we should forget what a lousy mother you are to your own kids,' Mum went on. 'I tell you, Lucy, I'd rather live in a hovel and dress Harmony in rags than put her through the torture you call tennis lessons and being-the-best-at-everything that you inflict on your poor kids!'

'Me too!' I grunted. I never meant anything more in my life.

'Shut up!' Aunt Lucy yelped, clamping her hands over her ears. 'Shut up! Shut up!'

How to transform Mrs Glamour into Pathetic Snivelling Wreck in one easy move.

'Yes, Jessica, just shut up!' Uncle Marcus echoed. Captain of Industry to Toddler with Tantrum. Magic.

'Take it back,' Mum said. 'Tell this woman that I do not drink!'

That was it. My aunt and uncle caved in. Sue Welfare made notes in her file. They all went away.

We haven't heard from them since. I haven't seen the Brain, the Brat, the Blub or the Blob. My days at Harris Palace have faded like a bad dream.

The ones I feel sorry for are Izzie and Jude. I only hope they get a new au pair as nice as Gabi, or else they'll turn out as mean and twisted as Luke and Bryony.

They need to play footie in the park. They need to stay as far away as possible from Aunt Lucy.

I worry about it, but Mum says you can't solve other people's problems for them.

Anyhow, from that day at the hospital, she

cut her brother and sister-in-law dead. I said I didn't care how many plasma screen TVs they had, or how many times they flew halfway around the world to Disney, I wouldn't want to live in their family – not for – well, not even for a date with Justin Timberlake!

It's four weeks later, and I'm building sandcastles. I dig a moat, the tide comes in and fills it, just like when I was little. Then the whole lot gets washed away.

Leo laughs.

You remember Leo? Joe and Gabi have brought him on holiday to Llandudno before Joe gets back to New Zealand. Gabi's got a new job with Joe's mum, looking after Leo.

This bucket and spade stuff is all pretty low-key compared to Mickey, though I have bought a new swimming cossie, which is one step up. It's a lime-green bikini with orange piping round the edges.

'Dig, Leo!' I say.

Leo goes crazy with his yellow plastic spade.

This time we're burying Joe up to his neck in sand. Gabi helps.

'Mind you don't throw sand into the poor guy's eyes!' Mum laughs.

She did her three weeks' convalescing in the Q.E., and here she is sitting on a beach in North Wales.

We finish burying Joe, and Leo plants a paper flag on top of the mound. Gabi grins.

And in case you're wondering, Joe has to go back home to finish college. Gabi hasn't made any plans to fly out to New Zealand to join him, so no fairytale ending there. Not yet. Mind you, Joe will be back at Christmas to see his mum and her new family, and I guess Gabi will still be their nanny. So watch this space.

The sea has demolished the last of our castles.

'Anyone hungry?' Mum asks.

She and I wander up the beach in our bare feet and buy fish and chips. We sit and eat them, watching the gentle waves roll, break and run up the sand. No surfing for Joe. He sits with an arm around Gabi, eating battered cod.

'Grab that towel before it gets soaked!' Mum cries.

I leap up and drop my chips. Doh!

We feed them to the seagulls.

Naff ending?

I don't think so. I'm back to normal – that's all.

HARMONY HARRIS CUTS LOOSE by Jenny Oldfield

Now that you've finished this book, would you like another book, absolutely FREE?*

Your opinions matter! We've put together some simple questions to help us make our books for you better. Fill in this form (or a photocopy of it) and send it back to us, and we'll post you another book, completely free, to thank you for your time!

Was this book...
( ) Bought for you   ( ) Bought by you   ( ) Borrowed for you   ( ) Borrowed by you

What made you choose it? (tick no more than two boxes)
( ) Cover   ( ) Author   ( ) Recommendation   ( ) Description on the book cover (blurb)   ( ) Price
( ) Don't know

Would you recommend it to anyone else?
( ) Yes   ( ) No

Did you think the cover picture gave you a good idea of what the story would be like?
( ) Yes   ( ) No

Did you think the cover blurb gave you a good idea of what the story would be like?
( ) Yes   ( ) No

Please tick up to three boxes to show the most important things that help you choose books:
( ) Cover   ( ) Description on the book cover (blurb)   ( ) Author you've heard of
( ) Recommendation by school/teacher/librarian/friend (please cross out the ones that don't apply)
( ) Advert   ( ) Quotes on the front cover from well-known people   ( ) Special price offer
( ) Being a prize-winning book   ( ) Being a best-seller

Which of the following kinds of story do you like most? (tick up to three boxes)
( ) Funny stories   ( ) Animal stories   ( ) Stories set in other worlds
( ) Stories about people like you   ( ) Stories about people with special powers
( ) Scary stories   ( ) Stories based on a TV series or film

How old are you?
( ) 5–6   ( ) 7–8   ( ) 9–11   ( ) 11–14   ( ) 15+

Name and address (in block capitals):

Please get a parent or guardian to sign this form for you if you are under twelve years old – otherwise we won't be able to send you your free book!

Signature of parent/guardian_____

Name (in block capitals)_____   Date_____

*Offer limited to one per person, per private household. All free books worth a minimum of £3.99. Please allow 28 days for delivery. **We will only use your address to send you your free book and guarantee not to send you any further marketing or adverts, or pass your address on to any other company.**

Please send this form to:
Reader Opinions, Hodder Children's Books, 338 Euston Road, London NW1 3BH
Or e-mail us at: *readeropinions@hodder.co.uk* if you are over twelve years old.

THE *DREAMSEEKER* TRILOGY:

Silver Cloud
Iron Eyes
Bad Heart

If you've enjoyed reading about Harmony Harris, look out for the *Dreamseeker* trilogy, also by Jenny Oldfield.

Winter is in the air and thirteen-year-old Four Winds' small band of White Water Sioux faces extinction. His grandfather, Chief Red Hawk, is close to death, and enemies hound them on all sides. A lonely vision quest brings help in the shape of the mysterious spirit horse, Silver Cloud – but at a cost. Four Winds must leave his homeland to fulfil three impossible tasks. Only then will his tribe be spared.